A Question of Will

Lynne Kositsky

Cover illustration by Carol Biberstein

published by

Printed by Brief Chronicles for
the Shakespeare Oxford Fellowship

In memory of Nathan
who shared my wacky sense of humour
and would have enjoyed this.

Thanks to Perin Westerhof Nyman for allowing
me to borrow her name; to Alison Newall for
her excellent editing; to Bob Barrett for comb-
ing so carefully through the manuscript and
offering such excellent suggestions; and to Jane
Frydenlund for taking the book in the first place.

Perin Willoughby

"I wish I could shut Peter Cross up. Stick duct tape over his mouth or something so he doesn't keep wasting our time," muttered Samantha venomously. The London sun was struggling to shine through the dirt-streaked window, giving her bright blue eyeshadow a deathly greenish glow.

"There's always someone like him in every class, forever asking stupid questions, paying no attention to the fact that the teacher's finished spouting like Free Willy and it's over," agreed Melissa. The straggly light in the room didn't do too much for her makeup either. The two of them were hunched on either side of my desk like Macbeth's witches (yes, we were studying *that* play) and speaking across me as if I didn't exist. That was no surprise. Since we'd been in England, hardly anyone had spoken to me at all.

"Look at his loser face. Why doesn't he just quit so

we can go on to something else, like a break for a Coke and a quick puff," sniffed Sam. "Did I say puff? Heavens to Betsy, that just slipped out. I'm as much against smoking as the next girl." She leaned forward and grinned at Melissa, who mimed blowing smoke rings through her orange lips. She looked like a goldfish with a headache.

But Pete Cross was still talking up a storm, so the girls' lung cancer would have to wait. I was beginning to get their point, though. "But Miss Smithson, I heard that Shakespeare didn't write those plays. He wasn't educated enough. Aren't we glorifying the wrong man?" Pete yapped. He was so earnest.

"William Shakespeare is the greatest writer in history, and you'd do well to remember that, Peter. All these stupid conspiracy theories are just that—stupid."

"Who cares? One dust-and-bones playwright or another, it's all the same to me," shrugged Mel. "He's been buried for millions of years, dog breath," she hissed in Pete's direction. "Who gives a hoot anyway?"

"I know that someone was the greatest writer in history, but I'm not sure at all that it was William," Pete went on, ignoring Mel completely, and unaware that Smithson was about to explode, blasting pieces of blown-up teacher all over the room. He stood up and placed his hands on the desk. He seemed set for a long siege.

"I need to go to the bathroom," Sam announced loudly to nobody in particular. Smithson glared at her.

"I need to check my lovely blonde locks to make sure they're still glued in place," whispered Mel into my right ear, thinking, no doubt, there was an empty space inside my head and her message would pop straight out the other side to her friend, who was examining a split in her blood-red nails. "If I'd only known that a summer course in

England would be such a blistering bore, you wouldn't have caught me here for dust or dollars. Mornings in class when I could be in dreamland, afternoons traipsing round one stupid site after another. And both me and my clothes looking like the Spadina streetcar's run over us."

"What a drag. I wish we'd stayed in Canada. You can't pack all those outfits into one suitcase without major casualties," responded Mel into my left ear. Maybe there really was a vacuum there. No wonder I was such a dummy in math. Face it: I was a dummy in just about everything.

Suddenly the classroom seemed smaller and pokier than ever. It was like spending my vacation in a coffin, and I was just about bursting to get out of there. "Miss Smithson, can we go now? I need a snack before our trip."

"Yes, all of you, go please. We'll reassemble here in an hour for our outing to the Globe. And remember, William Shakespeare was the greatest playwright that ever lived. I would be remiss in my duty if I told you otherwise."

Someone made a rude noise and we stampeded for the door; Pete stayed behind to argue. I didn't get what all the fuss was about. Shakespeare was Shakespeare. You did him in school (and on summer courses) because you'd no other choice, because you couldn't get into college without him. Mostly I thought of him as a boring old geezer, the author of a jumble of words I could only half understand on a good day with the light on. It was a puzzle. Why did Pete care?

"Hey, Willoughby Wallaby Werin, are you coming or not?" sighed Sam impatiently, rolling her eyes at Mel. But I had to be grateful for any crumbs of friendship I could get. So I was cool. I was loose. I was out of there, mingling with the pack.

John Pyke 2

Out of the mists of babyhood I emerge, riding on my daddy's shoulders, a giant among citizens and yeomen. Players before us strutting to a jig, spectators like a storm tide thrusting us forward, guffaws and snorts of laughter, foul stinking breath of the crowd. Will Shakspere a performer at the Stratford Fair this sun-washed day, and Rich Burbage too, still youths both of them, tho' ancient to my childish eyes. Pears and apples later, nuts and beer far my daddy This is all I will want to do now and forever: act. Such is my first memory.

Daddy succumbs during a plague year. Mother and I escape the pestilence, but she remarries where I am not welcome, and I am off to London to join the Admiral's Men. After one year's learning with Master Alleyn, a brilliant though unserious man who makes much fun of me, I hear Shakspere and Burbage are in town, and abscond to their new-formed Chamberlain's Men. An almighty fuss they make of me, of my talents and graces, my youthful genius in counterfeiting tragic and comic women, until a new boy, Willow, appears on the scene, the world goes dark, and I am all but washed up. Heigh ho.

3

I wanted to be one of the gang. I would have died to be, but as usual it looked like I wasn't a major hit with the crowd. I just wasn't clued in, decked out, glammed up or dressed down enough. My chest was still flat as a board with bug bites for breasts. My face was scrubbed shiny cos I couldn't stand the creepy feeling of foundation. I'd clump on mascara, then, when my eyes itched, I'd forget and smear it all over my cheeks. So I'd end up looking like a raccoon. I had to face it. In the clique's eyes, in mine too most of the time, I was hopeless. Five foot one and a quarter (maybe) in my Nikes, curly dark hair too short to shimmer, I majorly preferred baseball to rock concerts, hockey to raves. No surprise the terrible twosome and the rest of the class left me standing in their dust as soon as we reached London Bridge Station. They laughed wickedly as they galloped down the road. Smithson rushed after them, trying to catch up, her high heels clicking sharply along the pavement. In a moment, they'd all disappeared, and the road zigzagged dizzily in front of me.

"Walk to Southwark Cathedral and then west along the river," she'd insisted before we left, in case any of us got lost. I kept repeating her directions to myself, my tongue trapping the odd tear as it dripped down my face while I strode along the footpath by the Thames. Sheez! I was alone again. It made no difference that Sam and Mel were like cardboard cutouts; I'd be two-dimensional forever if only I could be one of their cronies. Pete Cross would accept me, of that I was pretty sure. He'd even hung behind a couple of times on trips to wait for me. But I'd avoided him. Who wanted to be the gal pal of a complete nerd?

I slowed for a moment, hesitated as I reached the bridge, then speeded up again: homeless kids, rough-voiced and angry, were quarrelling under the arch. Some of them lagged along the path, begging. One swore at me when I said I had nothing to give, and I walked even faster. Ugh, London was scary. The sun had given way to thick clouds, and there was suddenly a nasty sewer stench, a heavy dirtiness in the air like the sky was peeling. I choked as I tried to catch my breath. "West along the river, west along the river," I yakked to myself a hundred times before I realized I was moving forward in the wrong direction. Uneasy, I about-faced.

Now I knew where I was going. Or at least, I thought I did, though my right shoulder was pulling towards the sluggish water like I was being dragged into it. The Thames was a deep dark slate colour, the roads and buildings filthiest grey, not from drizzle or smoke or car exhaust, but from a spooky dimming of the light that coated my eyes like another skin. The sounds blurred too, like it was foggy—no traffic-roar, bird-chirp, or people-speak, and day was plunging into night so rapidly that the scene before me faded like a switched-off TV screen. Terrified, I tried to grasp a railing with my outstretched fingers before the whole of London vanished, and I grabbed...someone's hand.

"Mercy upon us," squeaked a voice. "It must be an eclipse." A boy's face loomed out of the blackness, immediately followed by the rest of his body. Tall to my short, fair to my dark, he was wildly dressed and looked totally weird. Perhaps he was an actor from the new Globe. Though his accent was unlike anything I'd ever heard before. Not English, not Canadian, the words fell from his lips in a kind of alphabet soup.

The day was now lightening like a bleached moustache, but there was nothing in front or behind us. Ever seen *nothing*? It's scary as heck. I clung to the boy for dear life, and he clung to me. He was clearly terrified, too. He obviously hadn't showered in a while, and though he was a younger, gorgeouser version of Leo diCaprio, my favourite film star, he was downright disgusting to hug. Swarms of dust flew out of him, and I'd bet a hundred bucks to a bee sting his loony costume had never seen the inside of a washing machine. How could he stand himself? No one had been that dirty since baths were invented.

More things were coming into the light, like a Polaroid picture developing. The stinking river was returning. The bridge was returning too, in the distance, and the pathway. There was just one teeny tiny problem. Everything had changed. London Bridge looked ancient, the buildings were hunched up and homely, and the taunting homeless kids had disappeared. There were still passers-by, but they looked way out and wacky. Even the weather had taken a cold leap towards winter, and I hadn't the faintest idea where I was. Maybe I'd gone through a wormhole, a tear in the fabric of time. Doggam it, I hadn't even the tiniest clue what century I was in. Was it the future, or the past, or the present on some far-flung continent? Past most likely, ancient history judging by Blondie's clothes and his state of hygiene.

I let go of him. He'd recovered a bit, and at least seemed to know his way around. "A thousand pardons," he chirped. After shaking himself down like a wet hound, launching a load more dust into the stratosphere, he moved on, making for the bridge.

There were strange ancient boats on the river, and ragged children on the footpath, pointing and laughing at me. Having no better idea, shivering, and completely at a loss for what to do next, I trailed the boy. I had to try something, anything, before I was whisked away again and maybe finaled my days on another planet. It was like one of those nasty nightmares where you're taking an exam and can't understand the language the questions are written in. Or where you're Alice running after the White Rabbit for God knows what reason, realizing at any moment you could plunge down a hideous hole.

"Hey," I yelled. "Hey, you. Hold up."

The boy ignored me at first, but I guess I was hard to disregard for long, shouting and puffing along behind him like an asthmatic poodle. He stopped and swung around, staring at me with eyes as blue as those man-made sapphires on the Shopping Channel. One thing you could say for him, though, his were the real thing. Pity he smelled so bad.

"You follow me, sir?" he cried out in his squeaky voice. Jumping jardinieres, he thought I was a boy! I looked down at myself. I had on all the stuff I usually wore: black leggings, a long white shirt and pointy-tailed vest. Skirts weren't my style. I suppose I could have looked like a guy to someone out of the loop, someone who didn't know what day it was, though it was a crushing blow to my all but nonexistent vanity.

The boy was dressed in dark tights too, with a longish brown tunicky thing over the top of them. They looked like hose and doublet. That's what Smithson had called them on our course. With his earring, arched eyebrows, and grubby cream collar, he resembled nothing I'd ever seen before, except maybe in a movie. It was probably better not to correct him about my gender. Could be I was safer male.

"No," I replied nervously. He started walking again.

"'Scuse me," I whispered, mouse-like, before he drifted out of range.

He made a fed-up sound like chalk squeaking, and stopped a second time.

"Could you tell me the way to the Globe?" Sheez, how dumb could I get? Here I was in the middle of history somewhere, still one rose short of a bouquet, and trying to find my way to a playhouse that maybe didn't even exist yet. In fact, everything was so weird, I couldn't even be sure I was in England.

"The Globe?" Not a flicker of understanding lit up those baby blues.

"Yes, you know, Shakespeare's theatre."

He must have understood that at least, cos suddenly he was making noises like a pop can exploding. "Will Shakspere, you mean? Certainly, certainly; you'll find him at the Theatre."*

Heavenly creatures, wasn't that just what I'd asked him in the first place? Now that we had something in common, he was eager to talk. "Walk over the bridge, up the street that leads off it—Gracechurch—and stick to it through Bishopsgate and Shoreditch Road until you see a big open area to your left. That's Finsbury Fields. Step by the two windmills, avoid the soggy spots and the arrows flying at you from all directions from the practice range, and pass by the first theatre, The Curtain, on your way to Holywell Lane and the second. Inside you should find Master Shakspere."

Well, he said something to that effect at least. He spoke so fast and furiously, and his directions were so doggam complicated, that I could barely make sense of them.

But one thing slammed me squarely between the eyes: my hunch was right. I'd hit pay dirt, been thrown back to the—pick a number—sixteenth? century, if his William and mine were a match. I was actually living and breathing the same stinky air as Shakespeare. But how the heck had I gotten here? And would I ever be going back? I felt like one of the crew of the Starship Voyager. Captain Janeway did this sort of stuff all the time. But I bet she was more confident than I was.

There was one advantage, though. Now I'd have something to tell that idiot Pete Cross about conspiracies.

*The Chamberlain's Men performed at the Theatre. It had no other name.

11

If I ever actually managed to get home, that is. Pete was obviously wrong, wrong, wrong! If Shakespeare really was working in a theatre, it made sense that he was the guy we always thought he was. He must've penned the plays! But the boy was still yakking. "I travel there myself, sir, and will lead you thither, if I may be of service."

"Right on," I replied, with a tad more confidence than I felt.

"I beg your pardon?"

"OK...yeah...sure thing...whatever...if you please." I hit on the right words at last. The lacy language would take some getting used to. But get used to it I would. After all, I had a bucket or three of time to splash around. Four hundred years, to be precise. Wow! The thought of all those centuries lined up like ducks on a shooting range made me giddy as all get out. But one thing occurred to me right away: there had to be a purpose to this. It couldn't all be for nothing. Could it?

John Pyke

October, 1595. Such a strange happening. On an errand to the Rose to see Jonson about a new play for the Theatre, the world goes black as a raven's wing, and I lay hold of a witless boy in my discomfiture. For a moment, nothing, an absence of all I understand, the city a wiped slate. I am brought back suddenly, but, having forgot my errand, I turn for home; the young one, still at my shoulder; accompanies me. Full strange he is, abounding with unfamiliar phrase, his apparel of foreign cut. Thin he is, too, but comely and quaint as a girl.

At London Bridge he starts in horror, almost swoons, the air mayhap too thick for him. In October, blowing east along the Thames, it gathers noxious seasoning between one place and another. I seize him again to break his fall. The child wants to see Master Shakspere, "if you please." Is this not true of every would-be apprentice? Every homeless or friendless waif who ever hailed from the provinces? Though truth to tell, we do need a new player since Doggy Peters—so named for all the doggerel he spake when acting—died of the flux last summer. A reminder. I was glad to escape Alleyn, the Admiral's Man, who called me pig, or pretty pig. Heigh ho.

5

I almost died when we reached the bridge. I mean, fancy coming through a breach in the space-time continuum to be greeted by such a disgusting sight. There was some kind of archway at the entrance, through which the boy and I had to pass. Stuck on sticks like broom handles, high in the air, were a dozen or so...well, at first I thought they were mouldy cabbages, but as we got closer I realized they were heads. Yeah, really, human heads, their eyes staring into space. They looked just like ventriloquists' dummies, except their ghastly green lips weren't moving.

I didn't know what to do first, pass out or barf up my breakfast, but the choice was made for me when my knees gave way. Luckily, Blondie caught me as I fell.

"Sorry, I'm always puking or fainting," I apologized. "It's a major disadvantage in life."

"Think nothing of it." He helped me back on my feet.

13

"Who in heck are they?" I whispered, as I recovered a bit. I pointed to the heads.

"Were they," he corrected. "Drunken tinkers, jarkmen, treasonous men. Morts, bawdy baskets and doxies, all privileged or lucky enough to escape the hangman's noose." Some luck! Avoiding hanging only to be beheaded. Rather like winning Lotto 6/49 the day Hydro has a nuclear meltdown. And I was still no closer to figuring out who the heads belonged to, or what their owners had done, though they sounded just about as vicious as our own swarmers, skin-heads, muggers, and Hell's Angels. The wind blew deathly cold off the water, whipping a smell of sourness and decay into my skin.

With an enormous effort, I managed not to gag up all my meals from the last three days, and we kept moving. The bridge was more like a mall, dense with houses, shuttered shops, and smelly-coated tradesmen, the road beyond almost as cluttered, passers-by as thickly packed together as a bundle of moshers at a concert. Tall buildings were thrust so close to their opposite numbers across the street that hardly any daylight squeaked between them. It was so dark I felt like I was trekking through a forest, and I'll bet if you lived in one of those homes you could have leaned out and kissed your neighbour's husband good night without leaving your own bedroom.

Everywhere was filth and rubbish. Great mounds of it were stockpiled outside the buildings, like it was worth a fortune or something, and a dirty gutter filled with stinking vegetable peelings and other frightful trash ran down the middle of the street. Every now and then, just to add to the squalor, some punk pitched a pot of yellow pee into the alley from on high. Holy Ravioli, did you ever have to dodge! Did you ever have to watch where you put your feet! It was all so revolting. When you took Shakespeare at school, teachers only told you how doggam incredible the guy was. No one ever mentioned he lived in the garbage dump from hell.

Why couldn't the fog return and swallow me up, then spit me back out in my own time? "Beam me up, Scotty, perleeese," I pleaded, like I was Captain Kirk in an old rerun. But no amount of begging would help. Everything still looked as large as life, the dirt if anything dirtier, the mess messier, a chill sun winking at me as we emerged from the awful hole of a city. After crossing a small section of what the boy had called Finsbury Fields, while the mud, like a monster from the deep, sucked down our shoes, I could see the two theatres quite plainly in front of me, round, flag-topped and colourful, almost like circus tents. I half expected to see a parade of elephants come lumbering out of them.

"That's where the Lord Chamberlain's Men work," announced the boy, pointing towards the second building.

We were actually on the verge of going inside. I was about to see where Shakespeare made a living. If he actually was the right Shakespeare, the world-famous one, the maker of the plays, I'd be the only one in my class taking an advanced course, even if I'd had to go backwards to do it. I couldn't believe my luck. Suddenly the bard didn't seem quite such a dreadful bore after all.

This seemed as good as any a time to tell the boy my name. After all, I really and truly appeared to be stuck here with no time machine and no return ticket. "By the way, I'm Perin Willoughby," I announced, sticking out my hand. The boy didn't seem to know what to do with it, so I shoved it back in my vest pocket.

"Any relation to the Willoughbys of Wollaton?" he asked.

"Actually, I'm related to the Willoughbys of Wallaby." He didn't turn a hair. "And you? What's your name?"

"Pyke," he replied, "John Pyke." We traipsed into the Theatre.

6

I'd seen models of the Globe in my course, naturally. And hey! who hasn't seen *Shakespeare in Love*? So I pretty much knew how this theatre would check out: a squarish bare stage with a tower, three galleries like upper-floor motel balconies for the rich dudes, and a big open yard where the groundlings supposedly burped, jeered, and spat. Everything was where it should be, all right. But what really shook me was the vividness of it, like it was in Technicolour. I'd kind of envisioned it in brown and white, but the Theatre walls were painted in wild hues, pinks, purples, and violets, and the stage was overhung with a canopy that resembled the night sky on Ecstasy: brilliant lemon moon and silvery stars against a royal blue background, with a great golden sun at each corner for good measure. And the activity in the place was awesome.

There wasn't a girl in sight. That didn't faze me, though. I knew women weren't allowed on the Elizabethan stage. Listen, even I had to pick up something from freak-azoid Smithson's dull-as-dish-water lectures. "Only men," she'd smiled, sticky lipstick smeared along her front teeth. Her mouth was red and thin as a mailbox slot. "Only men were allowed to act." And men there were aplenty here. Hopping around, messing with trap doors, learning lines from long scrolls and shouting them out to whoever would listen, or putting on and taking off bits of costumes without a shred of shame. Sheez, lucky I had a brother or I'd have been shocked out of my socks!

"Hey there, John Pyke," called a wrinkly little fat guy who'd been writhing round the stage ringing the tinkly silver bells on his wrists and knees, "Wherefore were you out this forenoon, when you should have been practising and perfecting? And whom bring you us today?" It took me a good ten seconds of wading through the wherefores and whoms to realize he was talking at least partly about me. And by then the moment had passed. John was already answering him.

"Rich Burbage sent me to the Rose to see Ben Jonson about a new play...for our company...although the playwright wasn't there. Or was he?" John Pyke looked confused for a moment, and a cloud passed over his baby blues. I guess he still had a memory gap where our time zones had collided. But I'll give him this—the kid recovered quickly. "Master Kemp, this is Perin Willoughby. Perin, this is Will Kemp, the best comedian and dancer in all of England."

"Do you dance, boy?" asked the weird monkey-like man, who sounded like a toad with bronchitis. He spun around twice before launching himself off the stage with a flying leap.

What a weird question! Best to take a stab at answering it though. "Well, I took lessons for four years," I replied seriously. I remembered my ballet-dancing days without affection. "So I suppose I can do a pirouette or three if I have to. And I can manage a mean salsa when I'm pushed."

"Good, good," said Will Kemp. Looking wildly uncertain, he took a step backwards, knocking into the stage and bashing his bells. I seem to have that effect on people. They just need to look at me to have an accident.

"And can you read, Perin Willoughby?" came a commanding voice from a door at the rear of the stage. A man strode forward, tall, handsome, compelling. This curly-haired dude just had to be Shakspere. I stood up straight and threw my shoulders into reverse.

"That's Richard Burbage, Perin. Our Hamlet tonight, and the best actor we have," whispered John Pyke.

What a letdown! But what a gorgeous dude! "Yes, sir, I can read," I replied, a bit crestfallen at not meeting the main man, but ready to try almost anything for the beautiful Burbage. Not what he pushed in front of me, though. It was in the most dreadful handwriting, the letters full of squiggly lines and long wriggly S's like serpents. The whole thing looked like a doggam game of Snakes and Ladders. I turned the page around and around and even peered at it upside down a couple of times. It still made no sense at all. But suddenly, with no warning, the Elizabethan world slammed into focus once and for all with a loud camera click, and the squiggles congealed into words. Millennium magic! Must have been. There was no other explanation. Cos I was here, I was part of a Kodak moment, and without pausing for breath I read Ophelia's speech from *Hamlet* like I was acting out Sandy in *Grease*.

When I'd finished, there was dead silence. Everyone just stood around staring at me. "Well, I suppose that's that," said Burbage thoughtfully, and my heart dropped into my runners. I must have failed his test. Not surprising really. I flunked almost everything. That's why I was at summer school in the first place. But the guy hadn't finished speechifying. "Elizabeth and I have a full house, counting our own children and the apprentices, as does Condell, and Heminges and his wife Rebecca have already birthed too many to count, with another on the way this spring. Why they would want to breed like coneys I shouldn't care to hazard a guess, but at any rate you'd better stay with Shakspere on Bishopsgate. It's not too far from the Theatre, though I don't know what he'll have to say about it. He hoards his privacy like silver. Perin Willoughby. What a mouthful! From now on I shall call you Willow. Good luck to you." He turned with a flourish and walked away, leaving me feeling like I'd been electrocuted.

Me, short and prickly, Willow? Bramble Bush would have been a tad closer to the truth. But I didn't care. Once over my shock, I was hugging myself like crazy. Because even though I was a visitor, even though I'd dropped out of the sky from the future, amazingly, and without any planning, I was now a Shakespearean actor, a fully fledged member of the Lord Chamberlain's Men. And, though they didn't know it, Women.

7

I was changing. I could feel it. The times were changing me. Already I was totally in my element. Apart from the stench and the mess, this century fit me perfectly. I didn't need a dictionary any more to understand what everyone was saying, either. Mayhap their lingo had shifted, or mine was beginning to. As show time drew close, John Pyke, who was to play Ophelia, took me up to one of the galleries and tucked me into a corner. "You'll be able to see everything from here, and you'll be well out of the way. I'm sure Master Burbage will figure out something for you to do tomorrow."

I was relieved he'd found me a safe perch. The audience were pretty ghastly. They rolled in like a stinking tide, pushy and loudmouthed. There was a bunch of screaming, spitting and nose-picking going on in the pit, which was out in the open, and stuff transpiring between guys and girls in the covered galleries that almost made my curly hair turn straight. I tried to look the other way, but the view on the other side was just as lousy. Pot-bellied beer bottles smashed against walls, a man peed in a high arc from my tier into the crowd, while a fellow who'd been standing underneath got a watering. He raised his fist and bellowed he'd come up and fix the villain who'd done it, and anyone else who needed a good clobbering. I shrank back. Yeesh, it was worse than Famous Players at the late show on Tuesday night. And to think my folks were always complaining things weren't what they used to be.

There was a sudden silence as an important-looking dude walked in, and the mob parted like the Red Sea to let him pass. An older man, his darkish red beard spattered with grey, he was dressed entirely in black velvet and extravagant fur. Lurching forward with a slight limp, he lumbered slowly up to the gallery where I was sitting. His feathered hat was slouched low over his face, but everyone must have known exactly who he was, cos, as he moved by me, a whisper rippled through the Theatre, like the wave at a baseball game: "De Vere is here, de Vere is here." The man sat down further along the balcony, and the mob soon forgot him, went back to their pushing, laughing, and yelling. He glanced down at them with a sneer. Who was he, this de Vere? I hadn't a clue, but he was clearly someone significant, so I scribbled a mental note to ask John Pyke later. Check out the guy's pedigree, as it were.

John Pyke had told me Will Shakspere—that's how they all pronounced it, Shack-spear—was playing the ghost of Hamlet's father. Afterwards, he'd count the cash backstage before taking me home. It began to spit rain into the open pit as two trumpets blared shrill and off-key, and the show started. The groundlings hunched against the drizzle as they quietened to watch, though there was still a sigh here, a giggle there, and a stack of naughty goings-on in the galleries.

A trap door opening, a cloak for-to-go invisible, a candle and mirror to make the guy look ghostly: this just had to be Shakspere. But as he ventured out you could see he was a wimp just by looking at him, his sandy brown hair and owlish look about as scary as a peanut butter sandwich. He turned timidly and trekked across the boards like he was on a Sunday School picnic. A drunken groundling stuck a piddle pail on stage, and Shakspere stepped in it. A great roar went up as the poor guy shook his foot dry and wiped it on the back of his cloak. Swearing loudly, he launched both bucket and contents into the crowd before leaving the stage on the run. This was my first glimpse of my boss, my master, the good old guy I was supposed to lodge with. And, if he was the Swan of Avon—that's what Smithson called him—then I guess I was Donald Duck.

The rest of the play passed without incident, unless you counted some idiot actor not knowing his lines and rushing backstage every three minutes to check his cues, and Rich Burbage losing his cool with a spectator. Burbage was playing Hamlet and had just stabbed Polonius through a curtain. The guy in the pit yelled, "Give it to him again, Hamlet, you lily-livered pansy," and Burbage crashed into the audience with his sword still unsheathed to go a round or two with his heckler.

21

"Get on with the job," cried another fellow. "I ain't paid a penny to see you filleting the customers."

"Just try and make me," shouted the handsome actor, dropping his blade and taking a swing at him. Two other players, the boy playing Gertrude and a rapidly revived Polonius, just about had to tie him up to get him back on stage, with Burbage still dragging his victim behind him. Once up there, the fellow kicked himself free and bowed like a trouper. The audience applauded like mad. From that moment on Burbage leered at him grotesquely whenever there was a breathing space in the script, all the while making throat-slashing motions with his fingers.

By the end of the performance, just about everyone in the play had been stabbed or poisoned, blood gushing from their bodies like fountains. Will Kemp, who had played the gravedigger, ran back and danced the most disgusting, well, dance I'd ever seen, tugging at his hose and making obscene gestures which hadn't changed one bit in four hundred years. He topped off his wild show with a gigantic fart that boomeranged round the Theatre, and, just like in the twenty-first century, the fans went wild.

I'd have done anything for my smug old teacher Smithson to have caught his act and seen his antics, though she'd probably have had a heart attack. The way she yammered on about it, you could tell she thought Shakespeare was a religious experience. But if she knew what stinky down-in-the-dirt real Elizabethan theatre was like, she'd for sure have taught the plays only to kids over seventeen, and then with the sort of stern warning you see on cigarette packs: This lesson could be, should be, and probably will be detrimental to your health.

Every now and then I stole a glance at the mister in black. He sat quietly through the play, seeming intensely wrapped up in the spectacle. Even when the show was finished and the audience stormed the exits, leaving a ton of beer bottles, apple cores and nut shells in their wake, even as the fall dusk began to draw in, and the drizzle quit, he stayed glued to his seat like he was waiting for someone.

And he didn't have long to wait. Through the gathering darkness, I could just make out Will Shakspere creeping up the stairs towards the gallery. He had exchanged his ghostly gear for doublet and hose, and he now looked sinister rather than stupid. Yeesh! I faded as well as I could into the woodwork as he moved by me. He was so busy taking care of business that he didn't even realize I was there, thank goodness, and as he snuck over in the spooky twilight to the man I knew only as de Vere, or Vere for short, I realized I'd have to stay hidden for the time being. And that was harder than you might imagine. Because I was absolutely dying to pee, and being freaked was making things a whole lot worse.

Shakspere sat down next to Vere, and the two men glanced around quickly then started talking in hushed tones. Like they were plotting to kill some poor guy, knock him off, have him pushing up daisies. I could scarcely see them in the dark, and all I could hear was the occasional meaningless phrase which drifted over to me like a soap bubble. "No more money to give you," said the man in black, as well as "done when it's done."

Meanwhile Shakspere muttered words like "hurry," "necessary," and "favour." Perhaps they really were about to murder some poor dude, and were fighting over a contract. But right at that moment I didn't greatly care, cos if they chattered on for even another thirty seconds, my bladder, which must have been about as big as a balloon by then, was going to burst.

I couldn't help it. I squealed with pain, and Shakspere jumped up like he'd been stung in the breeches. "Who goes there?" he called out. Sheez, he sounded so, well, Shakespearean.

Vere stood up, too. He saw me immediately through the gloom, and limped over and grabbed me by the ear. "Well," he demanded angrily, "well?"

There was no answer to this so I stayed quiet. "Who are you?" he went on sternly, his eyes piercing the blackness like burning coals.

"W-W-Willow, sir," I stuttered, luckily remembering my name.

"It's only my new apprentice," said Shakspere. "Burbage told me about him earlier. What did you hear, boy?" He was sweating like a hot water tank. So was I. I thought the pair of them were going to snuff me.

"N- n-nothing, sir."

"Sure?"

"Y-y-yes, sir."

"Down you go then, down you go. We may only hope you show in your acting a little more wit than you appear capable of displaying at the present time," remarked Vere. He turned away.

Shakspere considered for a moment. "The child may be of some use to us," he said softly to his co-conspirator, and a tingle of fear raced along my backbone as Vere glanced towards me again.

"Tell young Master Pyke to bring you to my lodgings, Willow," said my new boss. "I'll be along later. I have business to finish here first." Yeah, right. Without wasting an instant, I ran down the stairs and out of the dark theatre. Feeling my way to a reasonably private place inside a small stand of trees, at last, and with overwhelming relief,

I peed with a great ocean gush onto the grass. Then I stumbled back in to look for John Pyke.

8

Marching back along Shoreditch Road with John, who was clearly annoyed at having to babysit, I told him he made a terrific Ophelia. He softened up, grinned and thanked me. His voice sounded perfectly regular now, and, compared to the stench of the mob, he didn't smell too bad either. Everything's relative, I guess. Perhaps if I didn't have a chance to take a bath myself for a while, which seemed distinctly likely, I wouldn't be able to sniff his cheesy aroma at all.

"Master Pyke," I said, when we'd been walking for about ten minutes, kicking at the stacks of garbage that lined our path, "who was that limp-footed guy in the gallery? The one all the spectators looked up at?"

"That was de Vere, Willow, Edward de Vere."

"He seemed like someone special." A rat rushed from one trash mountain to the next, darn near tripping me. I shuddered, disgusted and queasy.

"You might say so. He's earl of Oxford, and Lord High Chamberlain of the land into the bargain. A very powerful man. Hunsdon's the Chamberlain, and a good patron to the company. But Vere is our true benefactor, the reason we do so well."

He smiled stunningly at me. I'd understood little of his message, having no idea what a Chamberlain was, or a Lord High Chamberlain either for that matter, except to note they both sounded like important dudes. But John Pyke was so enticingly cute, so film-starry adorable, that I altogether forgot I was supposed to be a guy and kept cozying up closer to him. And he kept sidestepping away.

"Pray give me an inch or two to breathe, Willow," he mumbled.

"No problem," I replied. I'm not slow when it comes to even a hint of a critique. I jumped back at once, leaving enough room between us for a bulldozer to barrel through. And that was a big mistake. Because suddenly two strange youngish dudes were trolling along on either side of me, like I was the smoked meat in their sandwich.

"Hey, pig, hey pretty pig, hey pretty prattling pig of popular appeal, who's your bodyguard?" one shouted over to John Pyke, his face menacing as it slipped in and out of the shadows.

"Get away from him; he's a mere child," called back John huskily, as he spun round and saw the two guys ranged around me. They looked just like Beavis and Butthead.

"Not your usual type of consort, at all, is he, Master Pig of Parley? How goeth the play?" mocked the second fellow, who must've stood at least a yard higher than me in his bare feet.

"What's your name, child?" asked the first, sarcasm dripping.

"W-W-Willow." I was getting used to stuttering. Fine actor I'd make.

"Pussy Willow, pussy Willow," the second guy taunted. He grabbed my hair and pulled it like he was making taffy, before John Pyke got to him and pummelled him almost senseless. A left hook to the head. A right jab to the belly. Ouch. That must hurt.

I threw my feeble fist at the first guy, cos how could I

leave the Pykester to go it alone with these hoodlums? The bum's thumb poked me in the eye, his brutish hand ripped at my vest and yanked me down.

"Base football player," the first guy screamed, like it was some kind of insult, and I almost laughed through my tears. Then John Pyke, furious at the jibe, got to him too, and, turning him by the collar, propelled him violently into a wall. There was an ugly pause as the two would-be warriors counted the stars they were seeing, then they staggered to their feet and vanished, zigzagging down the road.

"Limp-kneed lily flowers," I screamed out after them, all spit and swashbuckle now they'd gone.

"Apprentices with the Admiral's Men," remarked John sadly. "Another acting company. They're our competition."

"The only other gig in town?" I asked.

"As you say, Willow, the only other gig. They caught all their rubbish talk from Gabe Spencer, one of their partners in crime, and from Edward Alleyn, my old master." He dusted himself off and pulled me up. "Are you all right?" he asked.

"Yeah, I'm OK." I was dabbing my forehead, which was a bit bloody. "You don't have to worry about me."

"Sure thing," replied John. We ambled on.

9

After duly dropping me off, John Pyke split. The house was huge, upper storey jutting way out like a ship's prow, windows darker than doleful.

I tapped timidly. After a moment's muttering and pattering, a kid slid open the door and poked his nose out. The rest of him soon followed.

"Yes?" he asked warily, kicking one foot against another, and scratching his head like he had lice. He probably did.

"I'm s-s-staying with Master Shakspere."

"Oh. It's only Shakspere's brat, Mother," the kid yelled to someone unseen and, from the sound of it, far off. Sheez! What a welcome! They must've known I was coming. The little monster scraped at his arm, rubbed his nose, and yelled again: "I suppose I'll take him up." He lit a candle, and we crept up the creepy staircase as ghostly, shimmery shadows licked the walls. Once on the second floor, he scooted me into a chamber and skedaddled.

Shakspere's room was a disaster. I couldn't believe I was expected to live here. That anyone actually did live here. It looked like a landfill site after a nuclear war, and smelled like something exceedingly ancient had died. People were passing outside, tittering and whispering. The door opened and closed fast. I caught a quick glimpse of what looked like a million kids, all turning somersaults. I needed fresh air. I needed to pee again.

But if I'd thought finding somewhere to breathe or pee was a problem in this flea-riddled back alleyway of a room, I soon realized that was going to be the least of my woes. Cos when Master Shakspere tore himself away from his dealings with Vere and turned up drowsy and drunk at our lodgings, he threw me a crust to chew on and filled me in on our detestable domestic details. Seems he was supposed to share not only his food, not only his room, but a portion of his straw-filled bed with me. He scratched himself as mightily as the kid had, throwing off his velvet doublet and shirt, and prancing around the room before sliding between the sheets. I could see that he made a habit of sleeping in his nothings. Yeesh!

"Climb into bed, Willow, there's a good fellow," cried the boss. "Long day on the morrow."

"I'm allergic to straw, Master Shakspere," I moaned, my face firmly turned towards the little glass panes in the window. "I'll sleep on the floor."

"Nonsense, child. It's far too cold, and you'll catch an evil humour and die. Right in, right now, sirrah." His birdy owl eyes bored like drills into my back.

So what else could I do? I scuttled like a crab into the deepest darkest corner of the four-poster and hung there, my nose stuck out the side for breathing purposes, bolsters stowed around me like a fortress. But Shakspere didn't care in the least bit. In fact he didn't even notice. Cos he'd already blown out the candle and was dead to the world, snoring away like a doggam walrus with pneumonia.

10

There really were about a zillion kids in our lodgings, running up the stairs, turning over the furniture, dangling out the windows, and fighting with one another till the blood ran. Even so, Mistress Lewes, their mother and the wife of the owner of the house, managed to stay cool and keep everything spotless, tidy, immaculate, in apple-pie order. Which was to say clean, quite a feat really. But her sweeping and scrubbing clearly ended right outside of Shakspere's door, cos his bedchamber, as I mentioned before, was an absolute pigsty. Scrolls of old play parts, dirty hose, and pewter trenchers with bits of green mouldy food sticking to them lay scattered over the chest and stool. The floor was no better, strewn with filthy rushes full of who-knows-what stinking garbage. No wonder she didn't want to venture further. It was enough to make you puke. I trod on a full rack of fish bones one day, and sat picking slivers out of my toes for hours.

"You need looking after, boy," announced our kindly landlady, waylaying me as I finally limped from the house that morning. From that time on she was to give me the odd piece of bread and dripping when no one was around, and outfit me in an older son's hand-me-downs. So I could borrow jerkins, hose and doublets, stockings and hats aplenty till a younger son grew into them. It was marvellous to be mothered. But I could have more than done with a shower. I was getting to the point where I was giving off toxic fumes, and couldn't bear to stand downwind of myself.

"Water costs dear in London," said Mistress Lewes, when I asked. "Though I've no doubt you draw it from the well where you come from." She obviously thought I was some kind of country hick. "Just try to bargain with the water carriers one afternoon and you'll see what I mean. But I'll give you an extra ewer and basin, and you can wash yourself down as far as possible and up as far as possible. It's good to have a clean lad around for a change. Mine wallow in the mud all the live-long day."

Clean? I was so dirty I was sticking to my kit. And it was hard to wash "up as far as possible" with Shakspere around. But I gave it a try when he was snoring, and if I wasn't as squeaky clean and spotless as a showerstall, I wasn't quite as mucky as I had been, either.

11

"What would you say to French fries?" I asked John Pyke at the Theatre a few mornings later as I swept the floor with a twiggy broom.

"Sorry?" He was fooling around with a little white hound and going over the lines for his latest role, one of the princes in the tower. That would mean *Richard III* this afternoon. Sheez, the plays flip-flopped so frequently I couldn't keep them straight in my mind. No wonder some of the actors wandered round the stage like they'd been hit over the head with a baseball bat. No wonder sometimes no one seemed to have the faintest idea what was going on. Once even the great Burbage strolled around during a performance spouting lines from the wrong play. It didn't go down too well with the crowd. They'd already seen that one.

"French fries. You know: fries, chips, shoestrings, crinkle cuts, McCain's spirals?" I was fast running out of synonyms, but John Pyke's gorgeous blue eyes remained empty. "Potatoes, Pykester. Have you never heard of potatoes?"

"Oh, now I understand, Willow. You mean those filthy root vegetables Drake dragged back from the new world. All bumps and knobbles."

"Right. We could peel them, chop them up, fry them in the room where everyone changes, the tiring house, and then...flog them, sell them to the spectators." I was flat broke, always having to rely on that geezer Shakspere for a penny or two, and he wasn't exactly loose with his change. Just the opposite, in fact. I had to take matters into my own hands and make some cash if I harboured any hopes of a better life.

"We could wrap them in manuscript paper and call them chips in a twist," agreed handsome Johnny. Cute and approving, he almost always went along with my plans. No wonder I was crazy about him, flaky as dandruff whenever I espied his fair form. I liked him so much I'd even flirted from time to time with the idea of telling him everything. But I still wasn't sure enough of him. And I certainly didn't want to be out on the street if he went telling tales to the management.

"No one much seems to buy potatoes," went on John Pyke, interrupting my thoughts, "so they're cheap as dirt." The little dog danced round in a circle, chasing her dog-gam tail, then lay down next to him.

"It'll make a nice change for the patrons from fruit and nuts," I agreed, desperate to do something, anything to make a buck, and dying to relieve the monotony. I'd thought I'd be stuck up there on a stage right away, acting up a storm and charming the stinking spectators like my stunning pal, but I had another think coming.

My first job had been to hold the horses of the rich patrons during performances to make sure they didn't gallop away. The horses, that is. Lucky I'd gone riding at Sunnybrook Park a few times, so at least I knew one end of the beast from the other. And at least they didn't smell as bad as their masters. John Pyke told me that looking after the horses was how Shakspere got his start, and, judging from the guy's tremendous talent for acting, he should have stuck to holding the reins.

But just as I was getting the hang of the job and hadn't lost a pony in days, just as I was getting a thrill out of stroking their soft velvety muzzles and murmuring sweet nothings into their ears, just as I was getting used to everyone yelling "hold your horses" at me at least fifteen times an afternoon, I got promoted, and was assigned to collecting the penny entrance fees from groundlings who were incredibly loath to part with them. Cackling caterpillars, that was a job and a half, as you can imagine. It was like their cash was glued to their paws.

And, to make matters a million times worse, I was forever being told by every Tom, Dick, and Harry in the company to fetch, carry, and even wipe their doggam noses for them. I was their latest recruit, lowest man on the totem pole, and didn't they let me know it? So fried potatoes seemed like a good idea at the time. And, boy, after almost a week of Elizabethan food—bread, more bread, and stale cheese—I sure could have done with a hamburger on the side.

John Pyke was eyeing me sideways, like he was wondering whether I had anything further to contribute to the conversation. I hadn't. I was just about to go back to my sweeping and get it done so I could dash over to Cheapside for a pound or two of cheap spuds, when Burbage, accompanied by John Heminges, the actor who took care of the cash when my boss wasn't counting it, lunged out of the tiring house in a major sweat. For a moment I thought we'd been robbed.

"Seen Master Shakspere, Willow?" asked Burbage, his dark eyes flashing.

"Looking for me, men?" Shakspere strolled on stage like he was out for a country walk.

"The new play, Will. We need the damned thing so we can get it copied and begin rehearsal on it. You promised it for last week," said Heminges impatiently.

"Where's the bloody script, you twitch-tailed fly swatter? We need it now, this minute, yesterday or sooner," exploded Burbage, never one for understatement, "or we'll never have it ready for the Queen."

"Working on it at the moment. Not quite done," muttered Shakspere. And here was the real puzzle: in all the time I'd known him, I'd never seen him dip so much as a sharpened pen nib into a bottle of ink. You couldn't find a single sheet of paper or a feather quill where we lived, though perhaps that wasn't too surprising with the mountains of mess everywhere. And, when we were at the Theatre, Shakspere was more interested in playing cards with anyone who happened along than in penning immortal prose. He was the kind of regular mousy guy who would have been holding down a nine-to-five job and filling in *The Star* crossword at his desk, if he'd lived in the twenty-first C.

But what had any of it to do with me? There was no way I wanted to be involved. Around here, feuds could erupt into all-out fights in the wink of a blink. So I started sweeping my way to the other side of the stage. The little white dog, who was obviously running on a ten-watt bulb, growled menacingly and yanked at my broom like we were in a tug-of-war.

"This your mutt, John?" I demanded, totally bummed, cos the small mongrel had started to gnaw the broom handle, yapping at it meanly. I could still hear the quarrel rattling on in the background.

"Willow, meet Blossom, hound extraordinaire. You won't believe it, but this dog has more stage experience than the average apprentice. Brave as a lion she is, to boot." The squabble between Heminges, Burbage, and Shakspere went completely over the Pykester's head. He didn't tune in to them, just went on with what he was doing like nothing was up. Perchance he'd heard them shouting at one another a hundred times before and so it was no big deal. Me, on the other hand, they were driving crazy, nuts, mad as a March hare in April. I hated yelling.

"Hey there, ho there, Blossom," I murmured, pretending to feign an interest in his little mongrel. To be honest, I had no time for dogs, cos what were they anyway but expensive munching machines? I was a little scared of them, too. More important, though, at that moment I needed some quiet time, needed to get up and away from the angry yelling. But the doggam dog was holding me back, nipping at my borrowed hose and making a general nuisance of herself.

Meanwhile, the fight was swelling to a crescendo, with Shakspere clearly getting the worst of it. I almost expected him to take out a sword and skewer Burbage et al. with it if they didn't stop scolding him. But nothing half so spectacular happened.

"I'll see what I can do," he muttered at last, his bald head shining in the wintry sun. He crawled away beaten, with his tail between his legs. Now if only that little white pest of a dog Blossom would do the same, the day would be optimal.

12

"Willow, here," commanded the master, like I was a trained seal. He might have been a wimp when it came to dealing with his peers, but he certainly wasn't backward about being forward with me. "Come away into the gallery, sirrah. I needs must speak with you." I dragged myself upstairs, grovelling all the way, cos he wasn't above cuffing me if I was rude or slow. He hid us behind a banister and started to speak in low tones.

"I want a special favour from you, boy, but not a man jack in this establishment is to know of it. Do you catch my meaning?" It wasn't hard. I was sure the villain was about to involve me in some rotten scheme, most likely the one he and Vere had been hatching in the gallery.

I was still majorly puzzled when I thought of Vere, cos although he was obviously immensely popular with the crowd, and though John Pyke had given him a good say-so, he remained a sinister mystery to me. I thought back, remembering his visit to the Theatre. Dark, stooped and inscrutable, he hung out in the gallery like a mafia boss. I was sure that he, not my blockhead master, had to be the brains, the main man behind any plot, and I only prayed it didn't involve killing anyone. But it was a doggam freezing day, and I was rubbing my hands together briskly to warm them. Shakspere took my gesture to mean I wanted to get in on the action. He continued eagerly.

"Tomorrow morn, at dawn mark you, I need you to travel outside London to Stoke Newington, there to convene with the earl of Oxford. I have a message for him, but cannot go myself, being engaged in too many respon-

sibilities here." He puffed out his chest like a pigeon.
"Get it, sirrah?"

"Got it, Master Shakspere." There. I'd known right
away this was something to do with Vere. But the truth was,
I didn't get it at all. Didn't have the slightest clue as to what
I was supposed to be doing, or why I was doing it. I also
didn't have the faintest notion how to get to Stoke Newington. Travel plans always confused me. Witness my winding
up in the sixteenth C. when I'd set out on a boring school
trip to the new Globe. But enough of that. Though I could
recall my past, which, when you thought about it sanely,
would be anyone else's future, it was through a sooty curtain, stained and murky, and I felt freaky dwelling on it.

I slid back downstairs. The Pykester was hanging
around waiting for me with a fistful of playbills. We had
to plaster them round London to advertise the *Richard III*
performance later that day.

"Let us go via Cheapside," I advised, the doggam
puppy gnawing on my shoes like they were chew toys. I
gave her a sneaky kick when John Pyke wasn't looking,
and she bared her teeth at me. "That way, if you've got
some cash, we can buy some potatoes, and start frying
them up for the spectators."

"Sure thing," replied my friend, for the umpteenth
time that week. Another apprentice, a little prig named
Thomas, bent his head our way before getting on with his
work. I could have sworn he was listening.

And I'd have to warn John Pyke about tongue-tickling
a phrase to death. "Say OK, Pykester." He neatly obliged.
"Good stuff," I replied. "Let's go."

13

Though the roads were damp and boggy as a swamp, the citizens were out and hollering, bartering, buying, and whatever the heck else they did on a regular basis. We turned into the Poultry and then Cheapside, a broad and mucky shop-lined street with market stalls stuck higgledy-piggledy into the roadway among chickens, geese, and penned-up porkers. Those pigs were squealing like the world was about to end, which I guess it was for them. This was their last stop on the way to the butcher's and the great pie-and-pudding factory in the sky.

Sheez, the place was so crowded it was like the St. Lawrence Market on a, well, market day. Mostly it was foot traffic, peasants, housewives and the like, or enormous wagons rolling along the cobblestones. But an occasional rich dude on horseback swaggered along, a veritable rock star in velvets and lace, his servants running after him like the groupies that they were.

John and I tramped, poster-laden, from one shop to another, stepping around mud puddles and trying to duck the dirty great splashes the cartwheels hurled in our direction as they grumbled over the cobbles. We did our best to plaster our playbills to walls, though some of the merchants rushed out of their shop fronts, blinking their blood-shot eyes nastily at the sight of us, and shaking their fat fists into the ashy air like we were thieves.

"Buy my cloth, young masters, for a new jerkin or cape," cried a hawker as we walked past. "All the latest tones—puke brown, goose-turd green, rat's colour. Charm your lady friends with a doublet of dead Spaniard grey."

"Heavenly heck," I groaned. "Is the name of that colour for real?"

"Totally real, kid. Dead Spaniard's been the in shade since we defeated the Armada," beamed John.

"A farthing for a mouldy apple to throw at the stocks. A ha'penny for a couple of rotten eggs. Try your luck! Hit a prisoner," barked out a slimy-looking ruffian. You had to hand it to him. It was a great way to get rid of a cartload of groceries that were past their sell-by date.

A youngish woman sat locked into the contraption, her wrists and ankles poking through the wooden holes like spooky nightmare branches, egg-mess running down her face. "What did she do?" I asked the guy.

"Found masquerading as a gent, the shameless hussy. Fined a full shilling and sentenced to a flogging and three days in the stocks. Lucky she didn't have her hands and feet sliced off," he cackled. I gasped, almost crumpling on the cobbles, just as Blossom trotted over and began chewing the woman's toes.

"Call your bloody hound off of me," she shouted, a rat's tail of greasy hair falling across her face. My pal pulled the shameless mutt away, and, terrified, I fled quickly down the street towards Cheapside Cross. There I stopped, wrenching deep breaths from the dank air and thanking heaven I hadn't told the Pykester the truth in a weak but willing moment.

"What's up with you, Willow? You've been acting weird the whole a.m. And we haven't even finished sticking up posters," panted John Pyke as he caught up with me. His stupid dog was gasping at his heels like she'd just jogged a marathon.

What could I say? Nothing about being a girl, I knew that now. But the outing to Stoke was also bothering me.

The boss had been clear as floor polish that I wasn't to mention the trip to a man jack. Well, John Pyke wasn't a man jack. He was still a kid, like me. As we went to buy potatoes, those grimy root vegetables, all bumps and knobbles, that were going to make us filthy rich, I carefully told him everything Shakspere had told me.

"Take heed," he muttered, peering around like he was spooked. "We can't be too careful. The walls have ears. And the Admiral's gig is everywhere." He was acting like we were characters in a spy movie. But then, dontcha know it, the dear heart said he'd come along to Stoke Newington just for the ride. Awesome! Though I hoped that didn't mean he was going to bring busybody Blossom with him. She was getting the heck on my nerves and shattering my new-found moxie.

14 John Pyke

Late October, 1595. Outside Willow's lodgings on a cold and drear dawn at six of the clock. The child arrives tousle-haired and we set out for Stoke Newington. The way is long familiar to me. My family's domain lies beyond, near the southern gate of Enfield Chase, and we make good time tho' the path is mud-caked, rutted.

Not many abroad at such an hour; we pass a willing farmer and an early merchant, market bound. Blossom, my loyal guard dog, sniffs all comers. It will be rougher later.

A sealed letter in the fist of Willow for the earl, a mien of concentration for his task. Brave as a soldier, enchanting as a warlock is this fairy child. We banter back and forth in his outlandish parlance, for at last my tongue has

*caught the corner of it. I know him as a competitor, a dan-
ger to my ambitions, but he carries such a cuteness with
him, such a boldness of action, that truth told, I cannot
help but feel affection for the little fellow.*

*Arrived at de Vere's; his daughter Bridget opens the
door and I am lost forever, my heart only for her. The
most exquisite creature I have ever spied, petite, pert-
painted, and perfect as a goddess, she glides through
chambers of the house on business for her father. I wait
in the hall for a glimpse of her ethereal being, but the
hour grows late, and I must to the Theatre to counterfeit
Ophelia once more.*

*I bid the dog remain with Willow for his journey back.
I will wander along the road to walk with him when my
stage stint is completed, owing him this at least. We have
each of us harvested a groat and a penny's profit from his
fine idea of chips. Heigh ho.*

15

It was heavenly to get some time alone with the Pykester,
even if it was on a pretty gruelling trek through the coun-
tryside of merry England. By dawdling along the road,
I could stretch out the time I had with him like elastic,
despite the fact that horrible little hound kept howling at
my heels. And, for a change, the scenery was delightful.
No drifts of disgusting garbage like in London. No candy
wrappers, Popsicle sticks or coke cans, like four hundred
odd years in the future. Not even—dare I say it?—so much
as a used needle, an everyday find in the twenty-first C.,
littered the muddy route.

"Give me some air and stick to your own side, there's a good fellow," crabbed John, his breath blowing out of him in an icy fog. "Path's broad enough here for a dozen or so." I backed off grudgingly, the little dog shadowing me, gnawing at me, nipping at my long hose, my short hose, cape, cap, doublet and pouch. She just wouldn't give up. Even when I went behind some bushes to pee, the monster trailed behind me to get an eyeful. Lucky she couldn't speak.

"She likes you a lot," remarked the Pykester when I toddled back.

"She's got a funny way of showing it, then."

When we reached the earl's abode, we were greeted at the door by his dwarfish daughter Bridget. She was shorter than I, but I have to admit that, even under all those petticoats, she was better rounded, with bumps in all the right places. At the sight of her, John Pyke looked as though he'd been bashed over the back of his head with a frying pan. His baby blues practically popped out of their sockets, and my heart quaked, seeing him hot and hankering for someone else. But the lady didn't care one iota. She abandoned him and Blossom in the hall, and, as soon as we were out of sight, she sucked up to me like I was an orange, squeezing herself against my skinny body like she was trying to extract juice from me.

"Fair Willow, sweet Willow, young stripling Willow, my father has been apprised of your presence and awaits thee presently," she murmured breathlessly, her fingers running across my back like she was playing a piano. That was a relief, anyhow. The fact Vere was waiting for me, I mean. Radiated Runners, I thought I'd be stuck there in the alcove with her totally glued to me for the whole visit. Sheez, I'm a girl too, every pore in my body positively screamed at her, but she moved in even closer, and, for a moment, I was scared she was going to swallow me whole. A door opened, and she jumped back. It was Vere, ominous as ever, his dark eyes threatening. "You bring a companion with you?" The words were aimed at me. They slid sideways out of his downturned mouth, his lips a dark slash in the shadows. He must have spotted our arrival through a window, and was mad as a baited bear.

"Er...yes, My Lord...Your Grace...Your Eminence ...Your Highness-ship." My teeth were rattling together like dice on a gaming table. I glanced behind me for an escape route and realized that Bridget, who was clearly not as dopey as she looked, had disappeared.

"Sir will do nicely, Willow. Does he know why you're here?"

"No, sir."

"Why are you here?"

"I really have no notion, sir, except to give you this note from Master Shakspere. And my companion, John Pyke, has even less understanding of our mission. He indicated the way to your house, as he originates from a village somewhat north of here, but apart from that, he has no comprehension of my purpose. My lips were sealed. And thus they shall remain," I promised, as Vere leaned towards me, his eyes once more flickering with menace. But, despite my terror I almost gave myself a high five, cos I was definitely beginning to excel at speaking Elizabethan lingo. Not even the earl would ever guess I had popped through a time tunnel into his lap, so to speak.

He relaxed a little, and led the way into a great room stocked with dusty tomes. Off came the seal on the note, and Vere scanned the message in a second. "Blasted Shakspere! I was quite clear with him from the outset. What a goat-faced imbecile the man is," he bawled. "What a thick-tongued idiot, a clay-footed cretin, a nit-plagued nincompoop."

"A jumped-up jerk," I appended silently, judging it far better to keep quiet, for I was already, like it or not, the puck in the middle of their face-off. Instead I stood stock still in the centre of the room as the noble geezer reeled lamely around what I assumed to be the library. He was complaining bitterly, muttering oaths, and banging his powerful fist repeatedly against the book stacks. I admit it. I was shaking. He looked like he'd run a sword through a peasant or three in his time. But, "Oh, there is no helping it. I have so much work to do this day," he sighed with startling control after what seemed like an eon of obscenity. "You'd better take yourself off to the kitchen, Willow, and ask my daughter to fetch you something to eat."

Lunch with her ladyship? Not ruddy likely. The last place in the universe I wanted to be was packed into the pantry with her. She'd already pressed me almost to a pulp. But try telling her father that. So I scuttled out of his reach and back into the hall long enough to tell the Pykester I had to wait around till the earl dismissed me. John Pyke said he had to rush back to the playhouse in time to play Ophelia, or he'd be majorly out of pocket and in trouble to boot. But he left the dog with me. "Temporarily and for protection from them," he whispered, as he bid Blossom stay. "And I'll come back when I can." That was just dandy. The hound might possibly protect me from all the mysterious *them*, but who the heck was going to protect me from her?

I traipsed out the big wooden door with John, leaving it a little ajar, and watched him as he dwindled down the path. The dog whined like a lawn mower at his retreating back. Resisting an almost overpowering urge to kick her again, I growled like, well, another dog, and stared her straight in the eyes, whereupon she stopped making a racket. In fact, she started to pad around behind me with a loving expression on her squashed-in face. Would wonders never cease? She was gazing at me with doggy delight, like I was the kibble in her bowl, the bone in her backyard, the pull-toy in her park. Well, just so long as she didn't try to gnaw on me again. But where the heck was I supposed to wait now? Wanting nothing to do with Bridget, Chimp Woman as I'd named her, I tarried among the dead leaves, kicking at the grass and mulling over my options.

A flash of movement caught my eye. Vere was still in the library. I spotted him through the mullioned windows and circled closer to see what he was up to. He wasn't reading, that was certain. Inside, his body appearing even more warped than usual because of the thick, pebbled glass, he was scribbling away like the wind in a thunderstorm. I figured he was still mad, cos the hand not holding the quill kept banging down hard on the table, making all the papers shake. His face was red as the rind of an Edam cheese, and I guess he was still grouching, cos his mouth kept chomping up and down like he was chewing on a tough slice of salami.

What could the fellow possibly be up to? Writing his journal? Figuring out the household accounts? A third lame idea was taking horrid shape behind my eyes, but I didn't even pause to think about it. No time to speculate now, no time to stop and surmise.

I ducked out of sight behind a tree, cos holy cannelloni, who needed more of the earl's ire if he suddenly caught sight of me catching sight of him? Blossom ducked with me, which, when you think about it, was a pretty weird thing for a dog to do, and we sat down on the cold earth like we were on a picnic where someone had forgotten to bring the chow. It must have been way past lunchtime, cos my gut was rumbling like Mount St. Helen. Perhaps I should try to slip back into the house again. I could wait in the hall quietly until a servant strolled from the kitchen and offered me a crust. Or mayhap—aye, there's the rub—Chimp Woman would arrive first, and offer me something quite different. I didn't need her to bounce my bones. I decided to stay put.

But the lady in question was already drifting through the grounds in my direction, fluttering through the falling leaves like a doggam damsel in distress. She brightened immeasurably when she caught a glimpse of my bony body. I couldn't figure out what the attraction was, cos there was no way I cut a dashing figure, but I guess there's no accounting for taste.

In the space of a heartbeat she launched herself on me, kneading my skinny shoulders like dough and knocking me lengthwise. I was done for! Or at least, I thought I was, until Blossom, my newly faithful vassal, jumped her from behind. Snarling and gnashing like the hound from hell, the dog terrified the life out of Bridget. The girl was soon back in a somewhat vertical position, her white farthingale swirling out in the chilly breeze like a ship in full sail.

"Fair Willow, sweet Willow, young stripling Willow," she muttered bravely, putting her petticoats to rights, "will you not follow me in for a veritable banquet?" She kept a respectful distance after that, as well she might. And we sauntered inside for a snack.

16

Twilight was falling as I left, its shadows deepening the dark red-brown of the trees and shrubs. Vere came into the garden with me, passing me a package with the letters E.V. entwined on the cover. "Tell Shakspere," he gabbed, "dimwitted dullard that he is, to make the tit willow sing in this one." He made me repeat what he'd said a couple of times. I hadn't the faintest clue what he was talking about, but beautiful bonce smackers! At least it didn't appear to involve dead guys. Then he stooped down and patted the pooch, who rolled over on her back and pedalled her paws in the air like a doggam cyclist in the Tour de France. She stood up at last, licked him lustily, swished her tail jauntily, and we took off.

At first it wasn't too bad. The path was clear, and I thought of all manner of stuff as I trekked down the road, flinging the occasional stick for Blossom: how well the chips in a twist had gone down with the audience; how we could try sandwiches—willowiches?—next; how crazy I was about the Pykester; how mushy he got around Chimp Woman of the gruesome goldy locks. Ugh! Think of something else!

I was so lost in thought that a dense fog, scummy and scary, took me completely by surprise when it billowed up from the fields. The trees, houses, and bushes withered to phantoms, and night, creepy and quiet as a morgue, penned me in. Tendrils of mist groped at my eyes and ears, stopped up my mouth like mashed potatoes, and, for the second time that day, hard though it is to credit, I was grateful I had the little puppy person along to keep me company.

My pulse hammering, I peered at the vaguely familiar outlines, and made for what I took to be the southeast, remembering that I had to turn right at Shoreditch. But it was so foggy I probably wouldn't be able to spot a caravan of camels, never mind a pathway. On top of everything, I was absolutely exhausted, and Vere's brown paper parcel, which had weighed a feather at most when I set out, now seemed as heavy as a ton of coal.

Of course I missed the Shoreditch Road, and didn't realize it until I came to a row of houses I'd never seen before. I could just make out their candlelit windows like blinking eyeballs in the gloom. My heart sank. That meant I had to double back in the awful blackness, every step an eerie adventure into the unknown. It was like Space: The Final Frontier, though I had absolutely no wish to go where no one had gone before. For the first time, sharing a bed with owly-eyed Shakspere seemed a comforting prospect, even if he did strip, do the full monty, before leaping between the sheets, even if he did snore and burp all night long.

And there was something else: if the Pykester was coming back to meet me, as he'd promised, we'd likely wander past each other in the dark and never know it. But at least Blossom was thumping her tail, that was a plus, and the clever creature fluttered her rear end even harder when we hit a fork in the road. So I figured she knew whereof she wagged, and lurched left, which, by my reckoning, just had to be south.

Just then, I spied a couple of figures coming towards me, one of whom muchly resembled John Pyke. "Yo, Pykester," I screamed out, "I'm over here." Which was, to say the least, a major blunder. Something like unlocking a door to a crook, welcoming him in, and then handing over all of your hard-earned assets. Remind me never to shout out in the fog again unless I'm a hundred and ten per cent sure who I'm yelling at.

Beavis and Butthead, the two buffoons from the Admiral's Men, were upon me in an instant. "Hey, hey, hey, give it a rest, pond scum," I yelled, my usual cool rap deserting me as the first dude smashed into me full force, knocking the stuffing out of me, the second trying desperately to grab the paper parcel from my unwilling hands. I was so winded I couldn't even batter them back, just pitched around, punch drunk. A third dude, a full-grown fellow, joined them. He egged them on enthusiastically, jabbing the air with his fists, hallooing into the smoggy evening like a complete jerk.

Blossom, the bravest beast in London, leapt up and sank her sharp teeth into the second guy's arm, swinging from his wide slit sleeve like a trapeze artist. But the first guy was unstoppable, and bashed me so hard on the nose I almost passed out. As the precious pack fell from my limp fingers, the dog released her hold on the second guy. Then she dashed off with it like she was the mailman bent on express delivery. Which apparently was the right thing to do, cos all three dudes ran after her, saving me from instant snuffing.

Silence. I must have fainted from the pain, because I don't remember much. Or maybe I dozed off for a while. I think I even heard myself snore. When I came to, the fog was beginning to lift, and the road was as empty as a discarded beer bottle. Groggy as could be, dizzy and weak, I snuck behind a bush and lay there, too scared to move. And then I heard them. Footfalls. Muffled by the remaining mist. Getting louder by the second. My heart rocketed up into my throat, ready to bust.

"Willow," echoed a welcome voice. "Willow, where are you?" Sheez. Thanks be to God. It was John Pyke, the real John Pyke this time. I staggered back onto the road. "Who roughed you up?" he asked in horror, spying my cuts and bruises, my manglements. I recounted the lurid details, almost falling into his arms. Forgetting my gender completely, I gave him a resounding kiss on the cheek. It must have been due to the shock.

"Hey there, ho there, young fellow, give a dude some distance," cried John Pyke, still smeared with the remnants of Ophelia's rouge. How wacky everything was. He was totally a boy, girlish, and I was totally a girl, boyish. A match made in heaven, if he but knew.

"We were all so uptight," he went on. "Blossom trekked into the Theatre with a brown paper parcel, so I felt at once you'd been waylaid. I left the package and dog with Master Shakspere, and hotfooted it here. I'd have jogged all the way out to the earl's mansion if I'd had to."

I kissed him again, only this time right on the lips. He went red as a tomato and pushed me away. "Listen Willow, you've got to get this straight. You're a nice kid, but I'm just not that kind of guy. Get it?"

"Got it."

"Good." He offered me a hand and pulled me up. My knee was bleeding, and we stumbled back to my lodgings, musing on (1) why the two villains had been so keen to steal the package, and (2) who the third dastardly dude was in the trio.

17

"My feathers have been rudely ruffled. I was smashed like a veritable egg," I griped bitterly at Shakspere after the Pykester had left, as the boss rolled up my short hose and bandaged my leg with vinegar and brown paper.

"What...what has that to do with me?" he stuttered, angry and embarrassed. He got up and started stashing manuscripts under pillows, broadsheets under linen, knives under trenchers, nightcaps under cushions. Was he trying to hide something?

"Everything. You handed me a mysterious note, you made me journey into strange and unknown lands, you knew whatever I carried back could be hurtful to my health." Licorice lockets, that vinegar was some kind of punishment. It burned my cuts like blazes. "What was in the parcel anyhow, that was so all-out precious three guys were willing to fight me to the death to grab it?"

"Nothing whatever. It...well, if you must know, it was an accounting of the price we would need to pay to purchase a new theatre when the lease runs out on this one. A costing for wooden planks, paint, and so forth. The earl of Oxford often lends his expertise to the Chamberlain's Men on such matters. Perhaps those ruffians would be glad to get their hands on the budget to see what our plans are." He paused briefly. "Did he say anything of import, Willow? Any little significance for my ears only?"

"Yes, master." I couldn't resist. "He said, 'Tell Shakspere, dimwitted dullard that he is, to make the tit willow sing in this one.'"

"Well, well, well." The poor guy was working on it, trying to wring some meaning from the message, but he was also shamefaced, red as a clown's nose. He glanced up and caught me grinning at his embarrassment, so cuffed me lightly round the ear. Like I hadn't taken enough of a beating for one day. "Now, who is the master here, you or I? Get to bed immediately, sirrah, stop yammering on at me, and trust to God you will feel better in the morning."

A knock on the door. Mistress Lewes poked her head in. "How are you, boy? Anything I can do to make you more comfortable? A tankard of hot ale? A warm slice of pigeon pie?" I thanked her graciously but shook my head. It pounded like heck. 'With your permission, Master Shakspere," she continued, "I'll bring my broom and duster in tomorrow and give the place a good going over. We don't want any more fish bones lying around the floor, any feathered nibs or straight pins for the child to stab himself on. He is injured enough already."

"No, no, no, madam. I must insist you leave everything as it is. Soon you'll be able to clean this chamber clear to the wattle and daub if you have a mind to. For the moment I need my privacy."

"And your rent, Master Shakspere? For this month and the month preceding?" Now she was attacking on another front. She wasn't going to be outdone willingly. You could tell by the set of her teeth, which glimmered in the dim light like a row of buttered corn kernels.

"Goodness gracious, woman. You'll have the rent by Thursday week at latest. I've almost completed my new play and expect to realize a tidy profit on it."

"Very well. Thursday week it shall be, and not a forenoon later." Our landlady's head receded, turtle-wise. The door closed, and I was left alone with my boss.

Suffering sandmen! I scrambled into bed and tugged the sheets over my head before he whipped off his clothes, bombarding me with his birthday suit routine. And then I just lay there.

The old trickster was hiding something, you could bet your Bakewell tart on it. Though his explanation of the package did have a ring of truth. Especially taking account of the fact that the company were going to build another theatre eventually. I knew that from Smithson's lessons about the Globe. And Shakspere did say he'd almost completed the play, instead of gabbing, "I've done with it, Mistress Lewes. You can have your cash on the morrow." Like he might have done if Vere had just finished writing it and sent it to him. There was only one problem. And it was major. The whole doggam story just wasn't sitting in my belly right.

18

For a while, nothing much changed at the Theatre except the props and costumes. Burbage and Heminges kept hounding Shakspere about his play, and the geezer looked shamed, like he'd been caught stealing all the profits from a dozen performances.

Meanwhile, the weather had turned, and it was well and truly freezing. The street mud had hardened into a filthy-coloured ice rink, and we'd have to move soon, cos who in heck wanted to slide all the way through Finsbury Fields in November, especially when skates weren't invented yet? But the actors stayed on for the time being, and the weather made everyone in the pit and galleries shiver. There was only one plus to the terrible cold: people wanted to eat more to keep themselves toasty, and so we sold mountains of food.

John Pyke and I worked like slaves, keeping up with the demand for chips, and adding sandwiches to our menu. I put forth the proposition we call them Willowiches, because, according to my shaky time count, the earl of Sandwich hadn't been born yet. But John had a better idea. "What's that funny little name you call me, Willow?"

"Blue Eyes, Johnny Boy, Leo's Double?"

"No, none of those."

"Gorgeous, Blondie, Bonny Breeches?"

"Not those neither. Heavenly hamsters, kid, you certainly have a lot of nicknames for me."

I thought hard. Nothing occurred to me. Finally I got it. "D'you mean 'the Pykester'?"

"That's it," crowed the, well, Pykester. "That's what we should call those bread wraps of yours!"

"Wow, yeah! Great galumphing grandpas, we could call them penny pykesters," I laughed, "and the customers will come running." The next afternoon, a new gourmet experience was offered to the audience: we sold them beef pykesters, cheese pykesters, chicken pykesters, even, for the rich guys, pykesters on a plate. And, on Fridays, we sold fish pykesters with chips in a twist, because meat was forbidden fare on that day. We were well and truly on the way to making our fortunes. Incredibly thrilled, I jing-jangled my coins all the way home, though I first made good and sure to check the rival gig wasn't in the neighbourhood. Stashing the money in a pouch under my mattress, I took immense pleasure watching it grow into a tidy sum.

About a week after I returned from Vere's place, Shakspere came cruising into the Theatre like he was on a millionaire's yacht. "The new play, Rich, I've finished it at last." And he bestowed the manuscript on Burbage with a great many flourishes and a good deal of self-importance, like he was handing over the constitution.

"*Romeo and Juliet*; a fearful tragedie in several acts," read Master Burbage with great solemnity. "Just how many acts would that be exactly, Will?"

"Three or four," said Shakspere dismissively. "I've been so occupied I haven't had much occasion to count them."

"Is that so?" replied Burbage witheringly, like he'd caught the master in a whopper of a tall tale. Then, snapping his fingers, he swivelled round. "All right everybody. Places, please." And suddenly it was like a hurricane had hit. After all, it wasn't like the twenty-first C., when the whole thing would be keyboarded, then some lackey would just make copies of it. No. Scribers, shearers, scrollers, checkers were all scrabbling over one another and the manuscript in an effort to get underway. That play had to be hand-copied, cut up into various roles, curled into individual scrolls, and handed out to the actors in less time than it took to make a round of pigeon pykesters. Of course, that took a while—you had to catch the pigeons first.

As soon as Shakspere had received his six pounds payment, he started his usual beefs. This time, he was enraged that the scriber was getting more money for copying the text than he was for penning the darned thing in the first place. The boss said as much to Burbage, but the actor merely replied: "Stop squawking. He deserves double, just for having to decipher your scrawl."

Shakspere was furious. And he became even angrier. "Boy," he muttered my way as the scrolls were distributed, "here is your role." He clearly had no desire to hand it over. His eyes were scrunched up with reluctance, his face seething with strain.

I unwrapped my scroll. Sheez, it was long, very long, and I saw right away that I was to play Juliet in this fearful tragedie. There were her lines, interspersed with cues and the occasional sketchy stage direction. At first I couldn't believe my luck. The part had fallen into my lap like a ripe apple off a tree. How come? As far as I could fathom, I hadn't done anything lately that would persuade Shakspere to give it to me. But suddenly it all made sense.

"Make the tit willow sing in this one." That's what Vere had said. Of course! He must have written the play, I had to be the tit willow, and Juliet was the part he wanted me to play, or "sing" as he put it. Nothing else tallied. That meant that Vere really was the main man, and Shakspere just had to put up and shut up—in other words, do what he was told. But although in other circumstances I would have been thrilled, at the moment I was majorly unhappy.

It wasn't the part that made me feel like I'd just found a farthing and lost a pound—I was thrilled. I'd watched Claire Danes and Leo play Romeo and Juliet and die a hundred times over on my VCR, and I knew most of the lines backwards, even if they didn't make too much sense. And kissing the gorgeous Rich Burbage, who was playing Romeo, would be a major plus, even if it did smack a little of disloyalty to the Pykester. No, it was Shakspere who was bugging me. He was glaring at me like he wanted to cap me. I guess he didn't like being forced into things. And he wasn't the only one.

Arctic glances were shooting my way from Robert Goffe, and I figured out right away that his chilliness had nothing to do with the weather. He was an apprentice who'd clearly been counting on playing the female lead. And that wasn't all. There was a pile of angry actors pushed out of line behind him, each with a smaller part than he'd planned for. And all because of me. Cos I'd elbowed my way in at the top. Not a word was uttered. Not a sentence was spake. But it wasn't hard to guess what was going on. Even John Pyke was weighing his scant scroll with disappointment, though he came over and congratulated me immediately.

"Good for you, kid," he grinned. "I knew you could do it if you only hung in there long enough. My voice is beginning to break, anyhow. Some nights I sound like I have a frog in my throat, a bad humour on my chest. I'm playing the county Paris, my first man's part."

"Yo, Pykester, that's superior." I brightened a bit. "But if only we had someone to help us while I'm on stage, so we could sell more chips; and if only I fooled around with you and not Burbage in the play," I grumbled, "everything would be optimal."

"Cheer up, kid. We'll kit you out in willow-green with a wicked wig on your bonce, and you'll wow the yeomen from here to King's Cross." And, despite a few rough edges, that's exactly what happened.

19

"Where's your bum-roll?" burbled Burbage, examining me. We were in the tiring house. The tireman, whose job it was to guard the costumes with his life, and John Pyke, who was delightfully clad in blue, were standing next to my new Romeo. The three of them were eyeing me like I was some species of alien as I geared up for the afternoon's performance. And there I was thinking I looked so glam. All decked out in willow-green, as the Pykester had suggested, with a maide's-blush half-skirt peeping its pinkness through.

"My what?"

"Your bum roll, Willow; the cushioned thingy that makes your skirt, petticoats, and other sundry sections stick out," clarified the Pykester.

"Oh, it's here somewhere. I thought it was some kind of article to lean on." I pounced on the offending item and wriggled it under my skirt. "There. That better?"

"Not much," muttered the tireman tiredly. "Things'd fit a lot snugger all round, Master Willow, if you wouldn't insist on wearing your own shirt and russet hose beneath everything else."

"Well it's just too freezing to take them off. I'll get frostbite if I go bare." There was no way in Hades I was peeling down to my underwear for any dude, no matter how much of a hotty he was. Not even if he had lustrous curly hair and dark shimmery eyes like Burbage or blond locks and shining baby blues like the Pykester. Certainly not if he was as old and exhausted as the tireman. I simply had too much to lose. Besides, I was skinny enough to wear three outfits one on top of the other and still look like a strand of seaweed.

"It ain't no good, Master Burbage, I'll never make a credible wench out of 'im, but I done the best I could with what I 'ad," declared the tireman sorrowfully, like I was some manner of ruined painting.

"Tighten my corset if you're not satisfied. Though Jumping Jelly Beans, I can barely breathe as it is." Sheez, being a girl in this century was a real pain. The clothes were suffocating. And the thick lace ruff, stuck round my neck like a noose and stiffened with starch and cardboard, came close to choking me.

I did some adjustments, pulled, stretched, tugged and wiggled, praying I wouldn't need to go to the bathroom any time soon. It would be like trying to pee in a suit of armour. "OK guys, I'm ready to rock," I announced at last. "Let the games begin."

I'd rehearsed some, but I'd never actually acted on a stage before. The first thing that hit me when I walked out onto the boards was the smell and noise of the crowd. It was different from being among them, less disgusting and dense, more like a warm wave that washed round the Theatre, floating up to me like driftwood on a beach.

When Burbage first kissed me, I stared into his peerless brown eyes and just about swooned. Not cos of his technique, which was, well, technical, but cos a great roar went up from the spectators. He kissed me again for effect, they screamed louder, and I was hooked. It didn't matter that Bobby Goffe as Lady Capulet pinched and pummelled me every chance he got. It didn't matter that the Pykester was dressed up in that luscious Coventry blue which matched his stunning eyes. It didn't even matter that Burbage completely missed his footing during our big love scene and flew off the balcony into the arms of the dudes seated onstage, almost breaking his back. He could rise up and curse and yell, shake his doggam fist at the patrons as grimly as he liked. He could stab a wandering spectator or three instead of the actor playing Tybalt for all I cared, and he very nearly did. Nothing in the entire universe mattered but the hooting, howling, and hollering of the crowd. The roar of the grease-paint: finally, I clued in totally to what that really meant.

After I'd died, as Juliet of course, and smashed on top of Burbage, my bladder of sheep's blood punctured and pouring downstage like a clutch of scarlet ribbons, Will Kemp, who'd played Peter, bounded on. He pulled me upright, rolled Rich aside, and began to jig. Though I'd lately been dead as a doornail, worm's meat in fact, and this was a most grievous tragedie, I was so excited I started to salsa. Soon the entire audience were up and copying my moves, swivelling their hips and waving their arms in the air like a bunch of palm trees in a rain forest.

I glanced up into the galleries to see if the rich dudes were doing the same thing. And suddenly, in the midst of the raucous shouting, shrieking, and shaking, the thatched roof rolling and tossing like it was about to collapse, there was a resounding silence inside of me. Cos Edward de Vere, seventeenth earl of Oxford, was sitting up in the gods with a long-haired boyish companion, and he was staring down at me, amused, disgusted and disappointed. His eyes said it all. I stopped dead, and he tipped his black-feathered hat in my direction sarcastically. Sheez Almighty, he'd served me the role of Juliet on a platter, and I'd failed, flunked, bombed his test. I ran offstage and started to cry like the complete idiot that I was. And, to make matters worse, I had makeup on for the first time in months, so I must have looked like a doggam raccoon in a rainstorm.

20

Vere might not have liked me jumping around doing the salsa, but the rest of the audience and cast thought it superior. Trotting back to the tiring house was like returning to the dugout after hitting a grand slam, and my tears soon dried as I realized that I, Perin Willoughby, a.k.a. Willow, was finally flavour of the month. Vere was forgotten when, within the space of a gasp, Burbage offered me two other parts, Rosalind in *As You Like It*, and the littler Prince in *Richard III*. To be performed at Christmas before Her Gracious Majesty, Queen Elizabeth I. I was gobsmacked.

"You don't mind that I danced?"

"Not mind? Why, my dear young sir, I'm delighted."

"You're right. What can be better than a rousing romp for the ruffians after such a touching and tragic tale?" I boasted.

"What indeed?" He turned to take off his costume. Others crowded in to congratulate me.

Only Shakspere and Bobby Goffe lingered on the sidelines, but somehow that didn't daunt me, for who were they anyhow but a would-be scene-stealer and an annoyed apprentice? In any case, if Goffe was feeling unhappy, I could offer him a job selling chicken pykesters. I wriggled out of my willow-green and maide's-blush costume, taking care not to spread makeup over it. We all ended up at a nearby tavern and, after downing an enormous dinner and throwing back a tankard or three of cider with the Chamberlain's Men, I did the Ricky Martin thing again, shook my bonbons to the obvious delight of the crowd. Then I searched out Shakspere for the trip back to our lodgings. But he was with Ben Jonson, a playwright with the rival gig. The two friends were deep in their cups.

"Here," yelled Jonson, throwing me a penny. "Go your ways, Willow. Your master follows after." I said good night to John Pyke and raced back to Bishopsgate to gloat on my good fortune.

The house was hushed. Mistress Lewes and her many kids were asleep, and the boss, I knew already, would be a long time coming. It'd be at least another hour before he crawled home drunk. I stole up the staircase, the wooden panelling, much polished, gleaming at me through the gloom. The knob of the top banister reared up like a billy club. As I reached our bedchamber, I spied the faint flicker of light within. Had our landlady kindly left a candle to light our way, or was some dude loitering there, waiting to have a word with Shakspere? Only one way to find out. I trickled open the door.

Vere. Verily. Another of the brown paper packages in his hand. Lounging on the bed, wrinkling his nose like he smelled a bad, bad smell. Which, this being Shakspere's room, he did.

"Ah, Willow," was all he said, but he mouthed my name, sadly, slowly, and the air squirted out of me like toothpaste from a tube. My scrumptious victory in the Theatre crashed and burned. As usual, I was a flop.

"Yes, sir? Perhaps I offended you in some way with my performance?"

"No, child, not in the least; your portrayal was more than passable, though I never understand our custom of following a tragedy as painful and poignant as that of *Romeo and Juliet* with a prancing jig. Think of the message, Willow, the research, and the countless hours that contribute to the creation of such a work."

Wow! He'd admitted it. Or as good as. Hinted he was the playwright. Now I was almost positive he'd scribbled this play and all the others, too.

"I'll never dance again, sir, save for a comedy," was my only response, imagining this less of a giveaway than "Congratulations, sir, you're the toast of the millennium, the best doggam dramatist in the entire history of the solar system." But why, why wouldn't he be willing to identify himself as the main man? What game was he playing, and how long would he want to go on playing it if he could see into the future for even a single solitary nanosecond and glimpse that dolt, my boss, remade into the bard of Avon?

"Do whatever you're told to, whatever you need to, to bring the audience in," he replied, losing interest. He stood up and limped over to the window, steering around the disgusting mess in the room, staring out into the grimy evening like he was stuck in a spell. After resting his forehead against the glass for a second or three, he complained: "Now where has that duck-tailed dunce of a Shaksperson got to? I'm to meet up with Southampton again within the hour for the ride back to Stoke Newington."

Southampton? Was that the long-haired blond fellow? Weirdly, I felt a faint flare of envy somewhere deep in my gut, not wanting to share Vere or his secrets with anyone. I smothered the feeling fast. Suffering salmonella, the dude was old, ancient, forty at least. He was a one-foot-in-the-graver if ever I saw one. But he was also, no doubt about it, the most famous playwright of all time. And he was there, in the flesh, standing by my window.

Footsteps staggering up the stairs. A rumble like freight trains passing in the hall. The door swung open and Shakspere shambled in at last, steadying his swaying body on the edge of the bedstead. Staring sourly at Vere, the boss let fly an oath and collapsed on a pillow. Then he spied the package and as good as licked his lips at the sight of it. "Out, bumptious boy, out of here right now," he yelled at me, almost puking up his beer in his haste to get rid of me.

"But where should I go, Master Shakspere, in the middle of the night?"

"Go to flaming blazes for all I care. And no listening at the door, sirrah. Do I make myself clear?" He hiccupped.

"Clear as a country lake, master." I sidled from the room. Shakspere swung his fist at me as I went, but I ducked and he hit the bedpost instead.

I squeaked the door shut to the last half inch and listened at the crack, anxious to discover what was going on. It was hard to make out anything, cos the two guys' words were muffled. But eventually I heard enough to learn that Vere's daughter—could it be Bridget?—was to wed, praise the Lord, and here was a new play written as an entertainment to celebrate the blessed event. The information passed between Vere and Shakspere hush-hushly, between the lines, in secret code. But I was getting good at deciphering, and I sat in the shadows and smirked to myself. Hadn't I already guessed it, after all? This was just the icing on the cake.

A moment later Vere limped from the bedchamber, almost knocking me into the next century as he tripped over me and fell down. He remained kneeling, looking east and west along the passage before demanding, "What are you doing here, boy?"

"Nothing, sir. I fell asleep."

"Ah. A likely tale." He didn't seem in the least put out by my presence. Perhaps didn't greatly care if I knew his secrets, or mayhap thought I was too dumb to work out what he was up to. "By the by," he went on, "you are lodged in a Jewish house, Willow. Were you aware?"

"No, sir."

"The little candles in the window; the braided breads on the downstairs table. They are all a dead giveaway, as you would say."

So what? Why the big schemozzle anyhow?

He must have been telepathic. "The Jews are forbidden to live in England. And beware, sirrah—I once had business dealings with a Jewish moneylender in Italy. He almost ruined me. What can your master be thinking of?"

"I doubt he realizes, sir. He scarce notices anything these days. But, truthfully, the householders are kind people. Mistress Lewes often feeds and clothes me, and I won't believe ill of her."

"Mmm. We shall see what we shall see." He shifted, stood up squarely, and began to veer down the staircase in the dark.

I ran after him. "Sir, one question. Why did you want the tit willow to sing?"

"Marry, boy, because it's a wise, and a witty, and I'll warrant a wilful little battle bird." He frowned his farewells at me, and faded like a phantom into the night. Empty-handed. He'd left the package with Shakspere.

21

Bobby Goffe really hated me, that was for sure: he criticized and cuffed me every chance he got. Shakspere dissed me daily, perchance cos he'd been stuck with me, mayhap cos he feared I'd discovered his secret schemes. And I still needed to keep a sharp look out for that other gig, Beavis, Butthead, and Mystery Guy, at every turn. To cut a long story short, I felt threatened every step I took. At the house, at the Theatre, on the street, a mere whisper would twist my head around, a hint of a hubbub would set my heart to heaving.

And I was soon to be cut off from one of my few faithful protectors, Mistress Lewes, cos we were about to leave Bishopsgate for the winter season. The weather was foul, so foul in fact that the audiences no longer wanted to trek out to the Theatre. We had to move closer to the Thames if we were to make a living. So I was to lodge with the rest of the men at the Cross Keys Inn. We'd give performances twice a week, to practise before we went to the palace to spend Christmas with the Queen.

No longer would I have to room with Shakspere. It would be cool to forgo his immediate company for a fortnight or three, but I couldn't see how the move could possibly prove more murderous. Cos though I was to be the roommate of the heavenly Pykester, who I adored more than ever, the brooding Bobby Goffe was also going to share a bed with us, so my handsome winsome Johnny would have to sleep in the middle just to make sure I didn't get a major beating.

The day before we quit Bishopsgate, as I was cleaning

up the boss's clutter and returning some dirty dishes to the kitchen, I came upon Mistress Lewes in the downstairs hall. A letter in her hand, a tear in her eye, she sat sorrowfully on a stool as the kids tumbled round her like a bunch of acrobats. No way they'd get serious for a moment, even if the house was falling down. Doggam it, didn't the little nuisances have a school to skedaddle to?

"Why, what is the matter, dear Mistress?" I queried, pushing my way through the kids and patting the hand that lay stretched across the hall table.

"Nothing, nothing at all." She jumped up, stuffing the note into her bodice. But a small corner of it stuck out, and I could plainly spot the foreign writing scrawled on its tip.

"Mother's had bad news..."

"Today..."

"From her brother, Dr. Nunes..."

"And we shall all be in the Court of the Queen's Bench..."

"To answer to the charges..."

"Before year's end..." chanted the children. They were playing leapfrog, and didn't let up for a second.

"Fie! Judith, Jonathan, Jacob, not another syllable," moaned their mother, "or we shall all be undone."

"What charges?" I asked. But try as I might, I couldn't coax another word out of her.

"Mistress Lewes," I sighed at last, realizing the extent of the problem by the misery it was causing, "it's OK. I know withal what you're hiding, and am not alarmed by it."

"Uh?" she screeched.

"I know your secret religion, and I just wanted to assure you that it's all the same to me."

These friendly words were meant to calm her, but they

had the opposite effect. The lady turned green as grass and went into a complete meltdown. Collapsing back on the stool, her eyes staring wildly, she pulled the letter from her bodice and fanned her fevered brow with it, well, feverishly. Then bounding up once more, she began to stride through the hallway, colliding with kids and sideboards, shattering a bowl and upsetting a wooden shelf as she rushed into the kitchen. Tankards were toppling. Stuff was flying in all directions. Jousting junipers, what a racket! The pewter platters crashed onto the floor. Knives and spoons followed in a hail of metal. The kids stopped playing long enough to scowl at me. I guess I said the wrong thing.

She avoided me muchly after that. So now the score was protectors one, that one being my good old friend the Pykester, and bearers of ill will half a doggam dozen, at the very, very least.

JOHN PYKE

Early December, 1595. Pig in the middle I lie between Rob Goffe and Willow at the Cross Keys Inn, the first ready to murder the second for the least infringement of his rules or privacy. The bed is little, but the chamber clean, and, despite the tempestuous outbursts between Goffe and the frail fellow, it is a boon to lodge here at Gracechurch Street, where it runneth into Bishopsgate, far away from the cacophony of children and the prying eyes of my usual landlady, Rebecca Heminges of St. Mary Aldermanbury.

That small fry Willow keeps me passing warm at

nights, though I cannot persuade him to separate from his clothing. It is a strange and wonderful occurrence that a child so concerned with the cleanliness of others should be so imperfect in his own sanitary arrangements. He slides between the sheets full apparelled, as though anticipating fire, and he strives to keep the window yawning wide at night, despite the miserable cold, the risk of horrid humours, and our chilly protestations. Most detestable to Rob, for he cannot gain re-entry, the child attends for us to leave at dawn, locking the chamber door behind us; to piss in a pot, I trust, for he muchly mislikes an audience.

Driven to a rolling fury, more than once has Rob essayed to drag the youngster from the room or strip him naked 'fore he tumbles bedward. But truly, I do intercede, for the lad screams like a stuck pig, and well do I remember how pitiable it is to be little, torn from companions, without a family for comforting. And for myself indeed, I do consider Willow a smaller brother, obtaining some solace there.

We perform amidst the dray carts, hawkers, and other cozeners, twice a week perforce, because the intervening days are set aside by the innkeeper for other matters. About to imitate Ophelia before Queen Bess, I practise hard in our routine ads. For I cherish the honour, and do besides bethink me that de Vere's daughter will to court at Christmas, and so may soon espy me glorified.

The Admiral's Men, our naughty rivals, will also be there to compete and execute their plays. I will guard the littlest like a hawk to ensure he is not ambushed further. Though truly I do recognize it was the parcel pinchable, and not the pretty lad Heigh ho.

23

Staying at the Cross Keys while we practised for Christmas was a mixed blessing. For there in our shared bed lay the adorable Pykester, cuddling up to me between the covers, and I loved that more than I can say. But on his other side lay Bobby Goffe, ready to throttle me if I so much as crooked my little finger. He took up so much space, and pushed against Pykester so hard that, often as not, John Pyke had to shove against me. The force of gravity being what it was, I usually wound up under the bed.

John Pyke's doggam dog was driving me wild too. The Pykester had brought her along to play out a scene with Falstaff in *Merry Wives*, and the beast lay burping over our bodies all night, gustily sucking in the air that was meant for us and snoring it back in our faces like she was giving us some manner of present. I soon lost all my recent respect for her. No wonder the place stank. No wonder I wanted to open the window wide as it would go.

To cap it all, there wasn't enough room in the, well, room, with three kids and a duck-brained dog, to swing a plastic screwdriver. I ended up storing my borrowed clothes and my old gear on the windowsill, rushing to pick them up whenever the wind blew them onto the floor.

"Messy pig," muttered Goffe, bashing me on the head.

"Stupid monkey," I mumbled as Johnny jumped between us. Bruised and battered, I was more than ready to slug the idiot back, but he was really tall, a mountain to my measly molehill.

It was a hard life. I took off my togs and saw to other essentials when the guys were gone, but, pulverized pachyderms, they were nowhere near as stupid as that sot Shak-spere, and I had to watch out. One morning, as I lagged behind for a wash and change, Bobby Goffe trying to get back in and banging on the other side of the bolted door like he wanted to choke me, I noticed my breasts were beginning to develop. Hollering hurdy gurdies, that was a shock. They would give the game away in no time.

I rushed over to the window to find a cord among my clothes. I wanted to bind myself tightly so I wouldn't look so obvious. At that horrid moment, totally dismayed, I discovered all my gear was gone. Not a trace of it any-where. In fact, the windowsill looked tidier than it had in days.

This was just too much. Ready to scream, I searched round the room for something to stand on, so I could peer through the window and see if my things had dropped to the ground outside. They hadn't. Nothing down there but a grey patchwork of cobbles, half covered with snow. Sheez! It was the second time I was down to the tights and top I stood up in, and some of the missing stuff belonged to my landlady, Mistress Lewes. Believe me, after our last clash, I didn't want to watch her lose her cool ever again.

But that wasn't my main problem. No, I was in a panic cos my twenty-first C. leggings and vest were taken. Though I scarce wore them now, I always kept them clean and ready, toting them round with me like doggam good luck charms—my only hope of returning to my own time. I figured I'd put them on one day when the going got too tough, creep across London Bridge, and bingo! by some weird and wonderful stroke of luck or magic I'd suddenly be walking along to the new Globe to meet Mel and Sam. In my nice clean outfit. On a nice clean street. Under a nice clean sky. In a nice clean world. Except for the pollution, that is. Pretty dumb, huh? But without my clothes I felt ill-fated, like I was stuck in this stupid cesspool of a century forever. Like I probably had been all along anyhow.

It had to be Goffe. He must have stolen my stuff while I lay sleeping. He hated me openly, was out to get me any way he could. I threw my shirt back on and smashed open the door. "You stole my clothes," I screamed at the scurvy scoundrel, who was still banging. He reeled back in surprise. "You addlebrained anteater, you nut-cracked knuckle-duster! You purloined my possessions, heisted my hose, snitched my sneakers!"

He shoved his hands up to shield himself as I rained blows on his body. Then, "Don't be daft, Willow," he said as he whacked me in the stomach, "I never touched your attire. It wouldn't fit an undersized flea, never mind someone of my size."

I doubled over, totally winded. Meanwhile, the inn guests were standing round staring through the open door at us both like we were actors in an entertainment, which I suppose in a way we were.

"It's only those barbarians from the Theatre," muttered a tired-looking fat fellow, turning and tottering back to his bed, "wanting a bit of promotion for their performance this afternoon."

"Shouldn't be allowed out among respectable folks." His skinny wife trotted after him, and everyone else vanished.

"Yo, kids, what's this?" The Pykester arrived on the scene just in time to stop Goffe smacking me into next Sunday. He butted between us, plastering a hand on each of our foreheads and pushing us apart. Dogzilla nipped at our backsides. We separated. I was really glad John Pyke and the hound got there when they did. Or there'd probably have been nothing left of me.

"Now shake hands and say *pax*," commanded the Pykester.

"What's *pax*?" I stuttered.

"Peace, you dummy. Just do it."

"Say *pax* to that curly-topped carnivore? Never! I'd as lief kiss a toad," growled Goffe.

"And so say I. Amen." I gasped in a gulp or three of stale air, feeling really crummy. Goffe's punch had been a whammy. Pitching forward suddenly, I outsided my insides, throwing up into the flowerpot on the bureau. A disgusting smell assailed my nostrils and I sicked up again for good measure. Gross! Last night's awful supper, back for a rerun. We all left the room in a second.

"Now tell me the true tale," insisted the Pykester, his baby blues urgent as we squashed ourselves onto the stairway. Bobbie Goffe and I each volunteered our versions. Our stories were dramatically different, though, and Goffe, beast that he was, exaggerated his lies with all the googly-eyed frowns and nasty grimaces he could muster.

"So let's get this straight. You, the first party, Willow, insist Goffe stole your gear, and you, the second party, Robert Goffe, insist you're too big to fit into it, and why the heck would you want his grotty garments anyway?"

We both nodded, glaring daggers at the other. Goffe put up his fists as if to punch me, and I returned the favour.

Pykester glowered a warning at us. Then he wrinkled his brow, scratched his head, and tweaked his ear. "The answer's simple, guys," he proclaimed at last. "A hooker, well, hooked your habiliments, Willow."

"Huh?" I muttered. I hadn't a clue what he was talking about.

"In plain words, Willow, a thief took your clothes."

"A hooker?" I repeated, still stuck on the word. In the twenty-first C., that could mean only one thing.

"Sure. A naughty knave with a big hooked stick, who goes round lifting stuff out of open windows at night," said Goffe, delighted to have a defence.

"Why would he do that?"

"So he can sell them and make some cash," advised the Pykester.

"Oh," I said, weakly.

"Didn't we beg you to keep that window closed?" he charged. "But you would go leaving that latch unshut at every opportunity, and now look where it's got you. So shake hands, say *Pax*, and let's live likeably together...in peace...or I shall have to fetch Master Burbage to lay down the law to you."

"*Pax*," I muttered gloomily, taking Gaffe's hand like it was bathed in boiling oil.

"*Pax*, yourself," replied Bobby Goffe, touching my fingers like they were basted in bird droppings.

"That's right," said the Pykester approvingly, leading the way back into the bedroom. "Now who volunteers to empty the pot Willow puked in?" They both looked at me.

24

What a dump the palace was. Freezing and windy, filthy past any imagining. Toilets might be a good thing to invent, I thought, cos all those haughty aristocrats ducked behind the curtains for a quick pee whenever they felt the urge.

No wonder the Queen changed palaces more often, probably much more often, than her underwear. No wonder the courtiers zoomed round the castle circuit like they were race-car drivers. Every so often, someone had to scour out the stink.

Christmas. Or at least, one day later. The Chamberlain's Men definitely took a back seat to churchgoing. "It seems we have something in common, Willow," smirked Queen Bess after my first awkward performance. She patted me playfully with her perfumed glove.

"And what would that be, Your Highness...uh, Majesty...Your Queenship...Madam?" I stuttered. I just couldn't figure out what to call these dudes.

She moved closer to me, her teeth blackened gravestones in the boneyard of her mouth. "Why, sirrah, 'tis that we both wear a wig," she giggled gleefully, patting her fake red hairdo. But, shrivelled as an old walnut, her long white face wrinkled like a shirt that needed ironing, Queen Bess was sum-totally terrifying, like a body that had lain too long in the lake.

I tapped my long brown wig too, and she laughed at me. She was dressed in dusty black and white, and looked like a decaying chessboard. So did Bridget, her knee-high gnome-in-waiting. The courtiers, also dressed in basic black or dirty white, looked like doggam pawns in a *Through the Looking Glass* special. So we players in our riotous red, orange, green, and blue costumes really stood out as we swaggered about.

But Sheez, what the heck was Vere's daughter doing here? She'd already stuck herself to me like glue. 'Willow, thy wench awaits thee," she whispered coyly, after the Queen had waved me out of her presence for the time being.

"Sure...OK...whatever," I replied, scrunching my eyes shut in a vain attempt to make Bridget disappear. When that didn't work, I tried to slide out of her grasp, to little avail. She was so hopelessly tangled up with me it was like trying to muddle through molasses. Meanwhile, my crush, the potently pleasing Pykester, was trying to cuddle up to her. It bummed me majorly to watch him being such an idiot, particularly when he was frankly looking so foxy.

"Aren't you supposed to be betrothed to some poor swain, some earl, Bridget?" I asked her, as John Pyke shadowed her every step. Wow! What a bomb to drop! His blue eyes clouded, the Pykester looked woebegone.

"No, fair Willow, sweet Willow, young stripling Willow. Indeed, you have mistaken me for my sister. Promenade with me prettily, and I'll gladly show you the difference between us." Rats! I'd thought I had her that time.

Finally managing to push her away, and leaving Pykester to her tender mercies, I wandered off to quaff some cider and watch the Boxing Day revelry. An air of excitement swept through the palace as the Queen doled out presents to the servants. Old Father Christmas was hallooing in the entranceway, the Master of the Revels was deep into the wassail bowl, on his fifth or sixth cup at least, and the workers were lined up for their annual gifts. Jammed into the hall, jostling against each other in their haste, they anxiously awaited their rewards.

All this mirth and merriment just after I'd played Juliet made me forget for the moment how embarrassed I'd been. The play, to put it bluntly, hadn't gone according to plan. I'm ashamed to admit I wasn't paying perfect attention during the first act. Although I'd wanted to look luscious, I had an enormous zit on the end of my nose and had gone cross-eyed trying to get a good look at it. Before I knew it,

I'd stupidly snagged my willow-green and maide's-blush costume on a section of backdrop specially built for the show. Poor Burbage, playing Romeo, had done his best to yank me free, all the while spouting lyrical love lines. The scene was the Capulet's ball, supposedly Romeo's first sighting of me. After a few timid tugs, he yelled "Juliet" and jerked so hard that I flew into his arms with a terrible ripping noise, darn near snapping his skeleton, and sending him, myself, and the stage set sprawling. Taxiing across the boards like the US shuttle, skirt deployed behind us like a pink and green parachute, we narrowly missed an enormous candelabra, shot off the front of the stage, and came to a horrible halt in front of the Queen.

The other actors gaped at us, aghast. The Queen sat motionless. Juiced-up jackanapes, the silence was deafening. Until, that is, I managed to roll off Burbage and stand up. "Noble youth, thy passion floors me," I said. Not quite up to Vere's standards, but as good a way as any to break the log-jam.

"Bravo," cackled Queen Bess. "A ground-breaking performance." Wiping a gladsome tear from her eye, she'd examined me and the beautiful Burbage at close range, before telling us to get on with the play. What she saw must greatly have pleased her, cos we were firm court favourites after that. So I guess things weren't so bad after all, though I still blushed when I thought of us sprawled out under her feet.

Showered with sweetmeats, stuffed with sugared candies, I strolled back to my chamber later, my chamber, positively mine alone. For the first time since I'd been whisked back to this, well, backwater of a century, I had some privacy, could wash and change protected from prying eyes. And tonight I couldn't wait to get back to my little room and crow, proud and delighted cos the Queen had noticed me. Silly puffed-up peacock that I was, dancing along with no regard for what was going on, I let my guard down, noticed nothing amiss along the dim lit corridors till Goffe suddenly cried out behind me, "Beware, former bedfellow. Ruffians at eight o' the dial."

His voice vaulted off the grim grey stones. I slammed around. There, wedged between him and me, popping up again like dogammed jack-in-the-boxes, were my two old enemies, Beavis and Butthead. Back from a practice most probably, for their company's performance the next day. But this time I didn't wait to see if they had evil intentions, just swallowed my hatred of fights and went at them like a Rottweiler. I was really glad I'd made peace with Bobby Goffe when I'd had the chance, cos now he sided with me in the quarrel. By a happy circumstance, Pykester strolled along too, and we made mincemeat of the gruesome twosome.

25

"Entertain me, Willow, for I am sorely bored," babbled Queen Bess, a couple of days later, after I'd confused myself completely in *As You Like It*. I'd played Rosalind, a girl disguised as a boy role-playing a girl. A bit like my dogawful life story. Half the time I couldn't clue in to whether I was supposed to be upping or downing, coming or going, pulling on petticoats or puddling them off, and by the end of the play I was so bewildered I didn't greatly care. Anyhow, still a bit dizzy, breathless and exhausted, I was kneeling by the Queen's throne, cos that's where she kept me, like a caged canary, whenever I wasn't on stage.

"Entertain you, Your Queenship, Your Honour Roll, Your...?"

"Madam will do nicely, Willow."

"Madam, then. Entertain you? Gladly. I'll work on a mysterious mischief to marvel at, a sensational scene to suit." And work on it I did, until I came up with an idea that I knew would entertain her thoroughly, and might even put the competition between the rival companies to good use. I rubbed my bruises ruefully. I hadn't gotten away free and clear from our last encounter.

"Pick your favourite plays, Queenie, playwrights and players too, out of all the works the Chamberlain's and Admiral's Men have performed for you this twelve night. Scribble them down on a sheet of paper, seal them, speaketh not to a soul. And I think I can promise you a spectacle at the end of the season that'll make your hair, or rather your wig, stand on end." I outlined my idea. Her black little eyes gleamed like sun-dried raisins in the fallen bread dough of her face.

Picture it. Twelfth Night. Last evening of Christmas. After the final play is played out. The palace spruced with, well, spruce boughs. Holly berries, glistening mistletoe, garlanded on walls. A thousand candles twinkling in the great hall of the palace. Crescent cut-outs of moons winking in corners. Sunbeams and silver stars dangling from doorways. Lanterns suspended from ceilings. Pork and chicken pykesters on intimate tables set for four. Chips in a twist. Tomato treats. I gazed around and was thrilled. This was the perfect setting for what was to come. Seizing the moment, I jumped on stage. "Welcome each and all, Admiral's and Chamberlain's Men, Queen, courtiers, assembled company, to the one and only, the glorious, the grandest, the greatest show on earth: the superb, splendid, and sexy sixteenth C. awards ceremony—the Bessies."

The Queen looked up. She was grinning gummily as she ate her chips, though she seemed a bit upset about the tomatoes. Apparently, she thought I might be trying to poison her. I tripped offstage and whispered: "I found them in the kitchen, madam, all green and sickly looking. Verily, the cooks knew not what to do with them, but I dumped them in a drawer to redden. And here they are. An exciting taste sensation from the new world. Quite harmless, and decidedly delicious." I popped one into my mouth.

Following my example, she ate a couple, reluctantly, then scooped up a few more. "Go on with the show," she bade me peevishly, her teeth blacker than ever.

"Right now, Queenie, at your command." I sprinted back, glad to avoid my table, cos didn't you know it, Bridget was loitering there.

"Welcome to the first annual Bessies," I repeated boldly. "But before the main event, a delightful entertainment for your enjoyment. A big hand now for the Admiral's apprentices." I motioned to the kids from our rival gig. I'd been trying to get them to participate for days, which wasn't easy when we'd just thrashed the living daylights out of them. Still a bit wary, they glanced around, then took deep breaths, leapt up and began to jig, with a smattering of fal-lal-lals, hey-nonny-noes, and daffy-down-dillies accompanying their dance. Trumpets blared and drums thumped. A lute twanged in the background. Cooperation at last. I was stunned. Would wonders never cease? After they'd finished, we clapped enthusiastically.

Then my guys got up and joined me. In our knockout gear of top hats and tails, twirling our canes and tapping our feet, we showed the rival gig what was what. Bobby, John and that little grumbly guy Thomas offered the crowd a rousing rendition of "There's No Business Like Show Business," smiling majorly in the Queen's direction. Terrible Thomas kept falling over his feet and treading on the toes of the other dancers, so I made a mental note never to employ him again.

"Hey, Pykester," I muttered when John Pyke passed by me mid-dance, "Who's the fellow in the orange doublet, sitting second table over from Ben Jonson and glaring at me like he wants to throttle me?"

"Him? Oh he's an actor and wormy would-be playwright with the Admiral's. No need to bother your head about him." Pykester shuffled off to the right.

When we passed again, I whispered, "He's the moron who goaded the guys so they beat me up the night I returned from Vere's."

"Doesn't surprise me. Gabe Spencer's his name. Stealing's his game." And John Pyke looped left with Bobby while I rocketed right with Thomas, taking care to keep my distance from the little toe twinger. We whirled, twirled and bowed. Finished. We jumped offstage. The applause was deafening.

Now it was time for the actual awards. The Queen had given me a row of rolled parchments with her seal stuck on them, as well as a small number of statues in her likeness to present to the winners. Best costume, best set design, best wigmaker sped by in a sparkle, and we were onto the major presentations. The names she'd written on the scrolls were a mystery to me too, and I couldn't wait to find out who'd won.

"Best actor in a female role—And the Bessie goes to..." I snapped the seal, feeling a faint flutter, cos who knew? Perhaps I'd win this one myself. But no. "John Pyke, for his excellent portrayal of Ophelia." Pykester strode up proudly, and I gave him a statuette and a quick smooch before he could run offstage.

Edward Alleyn of the Admiral's Men won best actor for Tamburlaine, and I was very sorry, cos maybe it was my fault that Burbage didn't win the award. I guessed I'd slid him out of the running on Boxing Day when we both shot offstage. But without missing a beat, without wasting a word, I moved onto the crux of the matter: best playwright. The doggam seal on the parchment wouldn't break, and I stood there sweating as I tried to slit it with my fingernail.

"Ah, there you go," I smiled, relieved. "Ladies and Gentlemen, the Bessie goes to..." I glanced down, my eyes scanning the great name. Shuffling shish kebab, I just couldn't say it. Cos I just knew when he heard it, that smart-ass skunk bucket, my stupid boss, would proclaim himself the winner. "William Shake-speare, for *Romeo and Juliet*," I murmured at last, hush-hushly, but the whole audience heard and clapped.

Shakspere stepped up smartly, and I gave him the Bessie. Doggam it, I wanted to smash the statue to smithereens over his bald head. I wanted to flatten him like a fly on the wall. I wanted to scream out Vere was the real winner, not him. But of course I did nothing of the sort, just spoke smoothly, thanked the spectators for coming, wished them a terrific Twelfth Night, and split from the stage.

26

"Come to my chamber. I needs must talk to you," I told the Pykester a moment or three later, as we swallowed our dinners and marvelled at his prize.

"Now, Willow, none of your funny business." He bit into a chip, and stared in awe at his statue, a small black and white replica of the Queen.

"Naturally not."

"And you won't make a meal of me?"

I have to admit I was hurt. I'd never force my attentions on anyone, not like someone I knew. "I've eaten too much already, I swear, and I'm way too tired," I said, trying to sound casual. "But it's seriously serious so you have to stop by."

"Go on then. I'll join you soon." He turned to gossip with some admirers, and I made my way to my chamber along the long grey corridors of the palace. Away from the noise and fuss, how pleasant it was. My footfalls echoed along the stone floor, quivering the candles. I'd made my mark, no doubt of it, and Queen Bess was thrilled with me. Now I'd relax for the rest of the visit. Or at least, I could have done, if events weren't stacking up like a crash on the 401. Why did Gabe Spencer, that wormy would-be playwright, as Pykester termed it, have such an unholy interest in my comings and goings? And how could I stand by and watch that dreadful fellow, Shakspere, garner all the praise that was rightfully meant for Vere?

I opened my chamber door. Peace and privacy! what more could a fellow want? Kicking off my boots, planting the candle I'd brought from the great hall on a chair, I dropped down on the bed. I was well and truly beat, and if Pykester didn't stop by soon, I'd be fast asleep, no matter how pressing my problems were.

A shuffle, a mumble, and an icy air gust in the room. The candle flame fluttered. I sat bolt upright, shivering. If I had a dagger, I'd have drawn it. If I had a sword, I'd have swashed it. Cos someone was quite clearly lurking near my bed. Was it the scurvy wordster Spencer come to skewer me? A rival player, ready to run me through? "Disclose yourself, you jinx-eyed geranium," I yelled out, teeth knocking together, "or I'll wound you so terribly you won't know whether it's Twelfth Night or Michaelmas."

The wall buckled, and with a weird whoosh of air, a secret panel slid open. There in all her ghastly glory stood Bridget, her wrist ruffs blowing gently in the breeze. Where the heck had she sprung from? Why, I realized, the palace was probably riddled with tunnels, human mouse holes, rat runs, hamster habitats. Incredible, really, that no one had ventured by till now.

"Fair Willow, sweet Willow, young stripling Willow, you are the bravest and the best," she murmured as she strode into the chamber and, with a cunning lunge, swung her body, well, bodily onto mine, bouncing on my bones like they were a trampoline. One thing you could say for her. She sure was single-minded.

With friends like this who needed enemies? "Mistress, move yourself," I muttered, but she pretended to be deaf. With her paniered skirt, shift, and petticoats, her farthingale and bodice, her neck ruff, wrist ruffs, and pearls, she weighed more than an elephant. However hard I tried, I couldn't wriggle out from under her. So I grabbed hold of the bed curtains, trying to tug myself up and away, but they must have been hanging there for about a hundred years. All crud and cobwebs, they toppled down on top of us.

"Follow me, sir. I know a short cut," cried the lady, burrowing even deeper. Yeesh!

"Now, Bridget, this just won't do," I wailed at her in the dark as we tumbled around together under the bed hangings. The stale smell was awful, the dust close to suffocating. But after a coughing fit and an immense struggle, I managed to wriggle us both back into open air. I was still trying to free myself from her slippery grasp when John Pyke strolled in.

"Well, Willow, your bread certainly landed butter side up," he said bitterly, as he realized that Bridget, a.k.a. Chimp Woman, the apple of his eye, the object of his affections, was in bed with yours truly. He looked totally shocked, like he'd missed the boat and she'd sailed away on it. In turn she grinned back at him, her teeth gleaming in the candlelight like they belonged to some species of Florida alligator. With scarce a second's thought, Pykester made for the door.

"Hey there, ho there, Pykester, this is not what it seems. Get lost, wretched wench," I yelled at Bridget, "and bother my head, my bed, and my bod not a moment longer."

"I'm staying put," replied the lady smugly. Meanwhile Pykester had disappeared. I ran into the hallway after him. Chimp Woman hustled into the corridor after me. John Pyke heard the commotion and doubled back to face us. And there we all stood, glaring at one another like we were the three corners of some lousy love triangle. Sheez! Not to put too fine a point on it, I felt frightful. And Blossom, who'd trotted along behind her master, looked like the doggam square on the hypotenuse.

"I have to speak with you, John Pyke," I urged.

"Not tonight, Willow. I'm seeing the lady back to her chamber." He offered his arm to Bridget, she took it with barely a second's hesitation, and they strutted off together, their laughter rolling back down the corridor.

I watched them in anguish, then locked myself into my room, snapping closed the secret panel. With Super-girl strength, I stacked an enormous chest against it. It wouldn't stop visitors from strolling in. But it might slow them up some.

My candle winked out as I fell back on my bed. "Pykester, where the heck are you when I need you?" I howled. "I have to spill my guts to someone, have to tell all I know." But my pal had well and truly deserted me, and I was pretty sure I wouldn't regain his confidence any time soon.

JOHN PYKE

January, 1596. Damn and blast the boy! Angling between me and the lady, he steals all her fondness, captures all her sighs. She bespeaks me, but her fancy flies back to him in a minute. So soft with him is she, so wondrously well met, that I am like to puke in my beer.

And is it not the very dawning, the first light after my Twelfth Night triumph, that Burbage informs me my voice has grown so cracked I can no longer counterfeit a wench? I must content myself with minor men's roles for the nonce. Now I will see Willow prance, portray Ophelia while I rot as Reynaldo or play some other piffling part. The sot has stolen the Queen's esteem, my masters' good regard, the favours of Bridget, daughter to an earl. And I had thought

him always an ally, a companion, a true and trusty friend.
Woe is the day I ever took pity on the wretch, brought him
back to the Theatre to usurp my place. I have ever been
kindness incarnate. Now I am done with him for good.
Heigh ho.

28

It was snowing. That shark Shakspere and I had pushed off
from the palace on the tide and sailed back in a wherry to
the moorings near London Bridge. The river was bursting
at the seams, and our course was wild, the wet snow whipping at our faces and the wintry torrent splashing over us
in great gulps of freezing water. I was glad to clamber off
at last, while the wherry man tethered his boat, and wend
my way with Shakspere back to Bishopsgate.

Truth to tell, I was a bit more miserable than usual,
dunked in dirty water, dripping with snowy slush, dragging the heavy bags while my master journeyed ahead
empty-handed. At the same time, I was mulling over my
friendship, or lack of it, with the Pykester. Cos he would
have zero, zilch, de nada to do with me. Since finding me
in the arms of Vere's daughter, he'd ignored me totally,
and nothing I could do or say would change his mind
one bit. Oh, he was polite, doggam dignified in fact, but
distant as the farthest shore. I tried to win back his friendship by teaching him how to play baseball, using bum
rolls for bases. Mayhap we could challenge the Admiral's
apprentices to a game in the great hall. But he sighed
and wandered away before I was half done explaining

the rules to him. He didn't even glance back. I quickly clued in that from now on I was on my own as far as taking care of myself was concerned. And that was scary beyond belief.

I trekked up the street, tramping back to Mistress Lewes' house like some manner of page. In my master's steps. Where the snow lay dinted. Past the Cross Keys Inn we trod, and on to our lodgings. But by the time I staggered up to the door, lugging the, well, luggage, the boss had gone crazy, and was bouncing up and down in a frenzy. What the heck had I done now?

"I'm sorry to be slow, master, but this baggage is heavy as a month of Sundays," I cried, cringing from the slap which usually followed the storm.

Shakspere was steaming like a soup pot all right, but for the nonce it had nothing to do with me. "Look there, blithering boy, right there by the window," he raged, spit foaming from his lips. "Look there, there I say. Cast your eyes sideways. You do have eyes, don't you?"

I cast them. Rolled them round and round. Searched the length and breadth. Finally I came upon a scrap of paper screwed to the wall. I read it hurriedly. "The Jews have fled, gone from London, sent packing, and good riddance to them. No Jews wanted here."

Oh, no. One way or another, someone in the courts, a lawyer from the Queen's Bench, perchance, had caught my nervous landlady and her children, or frightened them to the point of fleeing. For the first time I understood her fuss and fluster before Christmas. Cos no matter how much fun it might be from time to time, no matter how carefully the nasty bits were hidden, this bygone world wasn't in the least like the one I'd come from. It could be mean, malicious, merciless. You might be rich one day and poor-housed the next. You might be complimented then beaten up in short order. You might even be beheaded at her majesty's perverse pleasure. Even if she grinned at you through her little loathsome fangs, even if she praised everything you did, it meant less than nothing. Living here was like clinging to a bleak rock in the middle of the ocean. In the end, most dudes dropped off and drowned. With ne'er a trace. And no one even sent a search party.

Shakspere was still trampolining, the bat-brained jerk. "To think I stayed here. To think I paid the woman rent. To think I laid my body down in this horrible house. Why didn't the quarrelsome dame warn me they were Israelites? Only think of the harm I could have suffered to my reputation, sirrah." That was so like him. He couldn't see beyond himself to their sufferings, their setbacks. At that moment I really detested him.

"Poor Mistress Lewes," I said. 'We'll never see her like again."

"Poor Mistress Lewes? Poor Mistress Lewes? Consider the trouble the mean-mouthed matron has put us to, boy. Nowhere to sleep tonight, for starters, nowhere to hang our hats, with the snow pelting us like knife blades. We'll have to tramp round to Holywell and beg Burbage to give us shelter. I hate asking favours of the fellow, but at least he lives near the thea..." He sputtered to a standstill, thunderstruck. "Goodness gracious! Devil take the woman! My precious papers are inside that abode, sirrah, Ungettatible at."

"Precious papers, master?" I stared at him.

"Yes, yes, yes, yes." The old geezer was wringing his hands in dismay. "The play, the piece...I... have...writ for the marriage of Vere's daughter...lies within, and I must get it, have it copied, apportion the parts."

"And what play would that be, master?" I pretended not to know.

"Uh? Don't bother me with details. We must get in somehow and seize it, or there'll be the devil to pay." He ran round to one side of the house then the other, glaring at the walls, gazing at every gap and crack, every nook and cranny he could crane his stringy neck into. "There you go, backward boy," he said at last.

"Where, sir?"

"Why, sirrah, don't try my patience. Scale the old oak tree, of course, and slip across to that second story window nearby. It's not mullioned, so when you smash it you'll have just enough room to crawl through. After all, you're such a skinny fellow you could squeeze in anywhere."

"Shakspere, you've majorly lost a slice of your pie if you suppose for one second you can persuade me to risk my life for a play."

"Nonsense, boy. Are you my servant or aren't you? Make up your mind once and for all, because, recollect well, trainees are ten a penny."

There was no answer to this, so I didn't.

"Once having gained entry, make your way to our bed-chamber and fetch the work in question. It lies within the chest near the bed. Then work your way out. Flingeth the play to me firstly, of course, in case ought should happen to you on your journey down." Cunning old geezer. He didn't miss a beat.

"And what's in it for me?"

"The female lead, beauteous boy, if you return to earth safely."

So yada, yada, yada, I did as I was told, though the window, when I finally reached it, was a about a mile too small. I climbed halfway in trouble-free but then got stuck like a size seven finger in a size five ring. Wriggling around like a worm on a doggam hook, I finally squirmed through, tumbling to the floor in a splash of glassy splinters.

Ten minutes later I'd found the play, but was still sitting in the chilly and deserted second floor hall, picking pieces of glass from my painful fingers. Sheez! In the shadows, I could just make out the title: *A Midsummer Night's Dream* by William Shake-speare. The small black letters E and V again appeared on the corner of the cover.

"What are you waiting for?" bellowed Shakspere. I hobbled over to the window and threw the book at him, if you get my meaning, then staggered downstairs and squeaked the door open. No way on earth I was climbing that doggam oak tree any more than I had to.

29

At last! I was to play Titania to Pykester's Oberon, a match made in heaven, or better yet, fairyland. Everything had worked out wonderfully well for a change. I got the part Pykester would normally have had. He got Bobby Goffe's usual role, and Bobby portrayed Puck, the pixie prankster who ran around making everyone in the play fall in love with everyone else. Thomas, the kid who should have played Puck, was left holding the horses for the specta-tors, and didn't appear on stage at all. Burbage tried him out as Pease Blossom, but he kept getting tangled up with his magic wand. "Are you sure I can't do it?" he kept whimpering. "We could try lopping an inch or two off the wand." Doubting Thomas we'd started to call him, cos he never took a word anyone said at face value.

But enough of the kid. I was dying to make a start on the play. We could practise till after Lent, which was a specially long time to prepare our roles. We could also try out a couple of performances in the Theatre for our usual audience. So we hopefully wouldn't turn the show into A Midsummer Night's Nightmare at the wedding of Vere's daughter.

It was dawning on me that in this play I might finally get to kiss the Pykester, even if he was acting unfriendly as possible, his voice as sharp as a pair of skate blades whenever he had to talk to me. He still helped out with the business end of things, but otherwise he kept his distance, though we now lived close by each other in St. Mary Aldermanbury. Shakspere had rented a room there when Burbage grew tired of us camping in his cellar, but the Pykester would never walk home or anywhere else with me. In fact, the only time we went out together was Candlemas, February 2nd. He and Bobby Goffe had a sudden fit of friendliness, or maybe they just wanted reinforcements when they ventured into the territory of the Admiral's Men. Anyway, they took me to the Bear Garden across London Bridge. The game plan was to see if the battle-scarred beast, who had been teased and tortured by a pack of dogs the day before, would lumber into the daylight and see its own shadow. If it didn't, spring would come early.

"Hey, hey, hey," hoed the Pykester. "It's turning, it's twisting, it's tramping out into the air." The sun shone suddenly from behind a cloud. "And...oh...mercy upon us..."

"Another bucketful of bad weather," yelled Bobby, spying the bear's murky shadow.

"Another six weeks of wretched winter," sighed the Pykester, shifting away in disgust.

I said nothing. While they were nattering I'd caught sight of Gabe Spencer, my old enemy, far off on the other side of the arena, and he'd seen me too, his eyes cutting through the crowd like a laser. I ducked down behind Bobby Goffe, and when I came up for air, something else had luckily caught Spencer's attention. Now his eyes were fixed on the poor old bear, which shambled about licking its wounds, dopey and dazed by the sun. I breathed a bit easier, and watched the bear too, though it saddened me to see it shuffling around so crumpled and beaten. For my money, groundhogs would have done just as good a job, and were smaller and tidier besides. The dogs wouldn't have been set on them either. Yeesh! Bear baiting! These people thought of it as entertainment. It made me muchly sick just thinking about it.

I was about to blurt my views out to the Pykester, though he probably couldn't tell a groundhog from a gorilla, when I realized he'd vanished, hotfooted it back across the bridge. Still angry at my supposed love tryst with Bridget, he couldn't stand to, well, stand next to me for too long, and must have taken off soon as the spectacle wrapped up. I threw a last long look at the bruised and baffled bear, a wary glance at Gabe Spencer, just to make sure he wasn't following me, and traipsed home behind Bobby. These days John Pyke was a serious pain in the butt, and there was little I could do to change the situation.

In fact, the way things were that winter I ended up alone more often than not, and certainly managed the main part of the shopping for our business on my own. I rushed around Cheapside searching for cheap ingredients while Pyke puttered around the Theatre and peeled potatoes, or fiddled around with the finances. And though I was bummed he treated me like an illness he'd catch if he came too close, I had to admit our firm was a going concern. We'd listed a couple of new items on our menu—hot daggers and hamburglars. We'd even hired a wench to come in and peddle our products while we were on stage. We gave the management a percentage of our sales, too, to keep them friendly, so the major actors were happy as toads in a rain barrel. Optimal!

One Friday in mid-February, I was rooting round the market haggling with the merchants for fresh fish. Making the most of the warm air that was gusting spring into London, I listened to the bird-chirp, smelled the snowdrops and daffodils. Peeping out wherever they hadn't been trodden into the earth, they sure were a welcome addition to the mounds of smelly garbage and other grunge on the flea-infested street.

Two dudes were wrangling somewhere far off. At first, I didn't pay too much attention as their voices washed around Cheapside, rising and falling, mixing into a noisy broth with sheep bleats, pig squeals, and pie men's patters. But a gang of passers-by soon gathered to watch the fray, and I was drawn towards them like a fridge magnet. After all, a furious fight was the closest you could get to sixteenth C. TV.

Punishing pounders, if it wasn't Ben Jonson and my horrible enemy Gabe Spencer, sparring like a pair of dog-gam prize-fighters. "Pigeon-toed pen pusher! Call those hen tracks of yours a play?" yelled Spencer, punching his companion in the ear, and whipping his velvet cape around like Zorro.

"Pussy-tailed part player! Second-rate scene scribbler! Couldn't scrawl your way out of a scrolled-up bog sheet," shrieked Jonson, who had clearly cornered the market on insults. "And acting? You wouldn't know it if you tripped over it." He smacked Spencer squarely on the nose.

They set to, the crowd clapping their every cuff, me trying to creep round them and out of sight, cos the last thing I wanted was another confrontation with Spencer. I wasn't stupid. Didn't I see the sword slung at his side? Didn't I recall him hollering and hooting as Beavis and Butthead punched me in the head that fateful day? Glaring at me angrily at the palace and the bear garden? I certainly didn't need another scrap with the guy, especially when I still hadn't worked out why he was so interested in me in the first place.

But barely had I skirted the crowd, barely had I set my feet on what seemed like safe pavement, when Jonson downed his fists and said in friendly tones, like the two of them had just drunk tea together, "Well, see you this afternoon, Gabriel. Must find an item or two for the weekend," and set out towards St. Paul's. Weird! As he stumbled off, I realized he was more than a little drunk, and so early in the morning, too. Suddenly, there was just a faint draft, a billowy breeze in the space where he'd stood, and a sighing of pent-up breath from the spectators. Now there was nothing but the smallest gap between Gabe and me. He was staring right at me. And he was still steaming. I could see it in his eyes.

30

"Ah, Willow," he hissed a second or three later, snatching me up by the scruff as if I were some manner of alley cat, "Wander this way, if you'd be so kind." Now that the wrestling match was over, the crowd was dispersing. The housewives were hurrying about their business. The merchants were, well, merchandising again. Darting my eyes around the jammed street, I realized no one was paying attention. I was invisible. Just another urchin. No protection anywhere. And the rogue wasn't about to invite me to a Valentine's party, either.

I kicked his leg hard and he groaned. I elbowed him in the belly, and he let go of my collar as fast as his pain would let him. "Stop that, sirrah," he screamed.

"Then leave me be," I yelled back.

Lobbing my basket at him, I made for Cheapside Cross, ready to clamber its heights and fight him off. But dontcha just know it? Someone had stuck scaffolding round it, and no wonder. Headless and hunched over, the doggam monument was collapsing into a heap of rotting stones. Spencer was pounding the pavement in my wake, so I ran towards St. Paul's Cathedral for sanctuary, passing gaping crowds of people, Ben Jonson among them. "Hey, Willow, wait up," he called, but I paid him no heed, just sprinted along the road. I was into the church safely, and up some steps, breathing a sigh of relief, when, in a horrible heartbeat, ghastly Gabe caught up with me, snagged me by my short cape, and stopped me dead.

"Hold on, you pennyweight of lard, you puppy dog's picnic," he sputtered nastily, dragging me behind a pillar. "Where d'you think you're off to?"

"N-n-nowhere, sir." Up close, his eyes were runny as raw egg whites, and gave me a crawly feeling deep in my belly. What the heck did he want? Why was he shaking me till my teeth rattled like tablespoons in a cutlery drawer? Why, in fact, was he after me at all? "We are in a church, sir. I beg you honour my right to sanctuary," I managed to spit out as he biffed me on the head. Yeesh! What a loser!

"That's good, very good, Willow, but there is no sanctuary, no safe place for you ever. My spies are everywhere. They watch your comings-in and your goings-out. Do you understand?"

I nodded slowly. Could I get away? I scanned across and over the long grey building, eyeballed up and down the aisle, but there seemed precious little chance of escape. And, if I kicked him again, kneed or elbowed the numbskull wherever I could reach him, he'd almost certainly whack me double for it.

He was hissing at me again, and I tried to tune in to his words: "And all because there's a little favour I want from you."

He, clear as contact lenses, wanted some kind of response like, "What favour, sir?" but I stayed stubbornly silent as he glared at me with those eggy eyes of his. He took a ragged breath, like he was about to swat me, then chilled and said pleasantly, "See those tombs up close to the font, sirrah?"

I turned to look at them. "Yes, sir."

"What purpose do they serve, my little man?"

My heart spiked. "They domicile the deceased, sir, dam up the departed."

"Uh?"

"They're for burying dead guys in."

"Yes, you nut-faced ninny, you cloven-hooved clod," he whispered. I could almost smell the saliva, like pond slime, dripping from his lips. "And that's where you'll be, my fine finagling fellow, if you don't give me all your go-between goodies."

"Go-between goodies?" I didn't have a clue what he was yammering on about.

He tried again. "Your parcels, sirrah, presents, packages, packets, plays which pass between the oafish earl of Oxford and weak-willed William."

Sheez Almighty, now I was truly stunned. The dog-nosed devil knew about Vere. How? How? And what did he want with the plays?

Galloping gobstoppers, what should I do now? Stand my ground till he strangled me, or agree to what he wanted, and then get out while the going was good? I was too scared to make up my mind. He started shaking me again like I was a pair of maracas. And maybe there were two of me at that, cos I was starting to see everything double.

"No, never," I cried at last. "I will never give you anything of Vere's. Do your worst." I drooped over like a limp lily, and was about to throw up on the villain's boots, really making him mad, when Ben Jonson rushed into the cathedral. He must have been behind us all the time. In a trice, he realized the mess I was in and shoved his bully-boy face into Spencer's, fixing him with his beery breath. "That's Shakspere's lad, Gabe. Put him down right now, right here, right this minute, before you do him a permanent disablement."

"In your dreams," retorted Spencer, rattling me like a gourd for good measure. "You're drunk as a sailor, you stupid sot."

"Me?" roared Jonson. "Are you talking to me?"

"Who else?" cried his opponent. There was a positively grisly pause. Spencer obviously wasn't in any way prepared for what happened next, just like I wasn't, cos he didn't even swallow his spit, just stood there like an idiot while Jonson whipped out his sword and stuck him violently in the shoulder. Gore spurted from the ghastly gash like sheep's blood from an actor's bladder. Spencer sagged to the ground in slow motion, letting go my arm in the process, and I stood staring at him, dumbfounded, as the red stuff started to seep in a horrid curdling mess down the stairs.

"Get out, boy, go home," snarled Jonson, giving me a shove. But I was stuck like cement to the spot. "It's all right," he went on. He ripped off Spencer's sleeve and used it to stop the blood. "The knave will survive...this time, I have no doubt." I roused then, and began to glide backwards towards the doors, my eyes fixed on the frightful scene.

"I'll get you for this, boy, have no fears on that score," gasped a white-faced and mealy-mouthed Spencer, a round gob of blood staining his lips. "Wherever you go, wherever you hide, I'll find you."

I jerked around and almost tripped on the steps, then flew down, taking them three at a leap. In a welter of fear, the sweat prickling my back like porcupines' quills, I pushed past the booksellers in the churchyard and ran all the way back to the Theatre.

"Yo, Willow. You're late for rehearsal," said Bobby Goffe, as I flung myself through the door. "If you don't take more care, boyo, Burbage'll lighten your load by a shilling."

"OK, OK. Give me a minute, Goffe, will you, to catch my breath?"

Pykester was peeling potatoes. Will Kemp was writhing rhythmically. Shakspere and Heminges were having a set to about cash with Condell, a hired actor. Thomas was doubting something. The tireman was rushing round complaining through a mouthful of pins that he'd done the best he could with what he 'ad, but the habiliments looked 'orrible. And Burbage was tearing at his handsome hair cos no one would heave to and help out.

Bit by bit, my heart stopped hiccupping, my pulse slackened off, and I ceased breathing in shallow halting gasps. I was still rehashing the scene between Spencer and Jonson, but I was here, I was home, and what had happened back at St. Paul's, horrifying though it might have been, was sinking slowly, thankfully, back into the sometime.

31

For the next week, all the talk at the Theatre concerned the fight. Gabe Spencer had been cut, Ben Jonson did the devilish deed. Gabe Spencer hadn't been cut, Jonson didn't do the deed. Ben Jonson had stuck that suck Spencer in the heart till his lifeblood ran out. Ben Jonson couldn't have done anything cos he was nowhere near at the time.

A boy had been spotted at the scene. No one was spotted at the scene, else they'd all know who'd done the dirty on Gabe. And who said Spencer was dead? He without a doubt wasn't. How could he be dead if someone had seen him sauntering round Smithfields only Saturday? Rambling round the Rose on Monday afternoon? He was sword-swiped in the shoulder, he was nippered in the knee, he was belled in the bottom, he was sliced in the somewhere unmentionable. All said and done, he was riddled with wounds too terrible to talk about.

And he wasn't talking. Neither was I. Worn out by all the gossip, I bit my tongue. There was no way I wanted to be dragged into the centre of the saga. I was in enough of a scrape as it was. In fact, glorious grumble bunnies, if and when Spencer came looking for me, I'd be in a major jam.

"Trouble is," said Burbage, as we all sat round a big trestle table at the Theatre on Shrove Tuesday, munching on a tremendous feast, "those two, Gabe and Ben, are a combination of bad blood and blood brotherhood. No good will come of this, mark my words." He swigged down his ale and stuffed a sausage into his mouth. Yeesh! Cholesterol city!

"You're a fine one to talk, Rich, you ding dong. Your own family is hot as a branding iron. Didn't your father brain his own partner? Didn't you attack his widow and her cronies when they came to collect, hitting them over the head with one end of a broom while sweeping them out of the Theatre with the other? No, no, no, you can't come the innocent with me," yelled Shakspere, who was packing in pancakes like there was no tomorrow.

Burbage, waxing dangerous, banged down his beer bottle and blasted out of his seat. "Shut your mouth, you weak-kneed warbler, you blundering backbiter. Wasn't it you put some flimsy fellow in fear of death and mutilation just the other day? And aren't you under a bond to keep the peace, you boil-bellied bite of bacon as ever chanced along to be my partner?"

"More verbiage from Burbage," growled Goffe grimly. "More swill from Will."

They ignored the apprentice. Shaking like Jell-O, Shakspere swallowed his last pancake and staggered up slowly. Facing the handsome Rich, he made a very lewd gesture. Sheez! Even I understood what he meant. This was shaping up ugly as the encounter at St. Paul's. Still freaked out from the first fight, I was out of my chair and cowering under the table in an instant.

"Now, now, now," cautioned Will Kemp, lurching to his feet and waving a ham bone in the air like a cheerleader's baton, "I pray you rest, good gentlemen, and eat, eat, eat. That's the whole point of Shrovetide. Stuff yourselves silly and then blow a burp from every orifice to stave off all the evil spirits in England. We have lamb, we have fritters, we have oranges. We have eggs, we have jam tarts, we have custards. We have hens, we have beef, we have peascod. Make you merry, masters. The hour is at hand."

"Kemp is right," cried Heminges. "Eat everything in front of you, and be quick about it. Remember well, we have a wild and woolly show to perform this day."

I slid back into my seat. With a splendid sigh, Burbage bounded back to his, all argument forgotten. Only my bumbling boss was left standing. "Sorry," whined the wimp, creeping back to his place. "Sorry, sorry, sorry."

"Of all the days in the year," Burbage babbled, totally ignoring his partner and chowing down on a chicken leg, "I detest this one the most. Pray God the trade apprentices will not come a-calling."

The Pykester, who was pigging out at the other end of the trestle table, near choked at Burbage's words. "I do recall how rowdy runs the house at Shrovetide," he noted. "Last year we were near toppled by that turnip-load of tricksters."

The company wagged their heads in agreement, still cramming cakes and cabbage into their mouths. I didn't have a clue what they were moaning about, so when we finished the feast and were clearing the table, I asked John Pyke.

"You'll find out soon enough," he muttered nastily, folding up the trestle and pushing it against the wall. "Hang on to your hose, kid. It's going to be a bumpy ride."

"Pykester," I begged. "Isn't it about time we buried the hatchet?"

"Huh?"

"Made friends again. Recronified. Bridget's not going to pal up with you or me in the long run. You can bet your bottom dollar that when the time comes she's going to marry a marquis."

"So sayeth you. Go play your doggam part." He strode off across the stage. Gloomily, I went to change into my costume.

Half an hour later, the pit was packed with trade apprentices, butchers' and bakers' boys, blacksmiths and the like, even rowdier than our usual audience. Yelling and singing, drunk and disordered, they had roared into the Theatre like a flash flood. Snorting and screaming with laughter, banging drums and smashing saucepans, they were clearly ripe for a riot. I shook in my shoes as I stumbled on stage. My first Ophelia, and it was a nightmare, like riding out a twister in a tugboat.

"No," shouted a scrawny fellow, pelting me with chicken pykesters. "We want you to play Hamlet, not Ophelia." I gasped and almost barfed into the crowd.

"And you, Burbage," yelled a knave who had leapt on stage, pots and pans dangling from his arms and banging against his body as he moved, "we want you to act out the wench." He pointed at the handsome actor, who was sweating big bucketfuls of, well, sweat. "Swap clothes with the boy, or we'll axe your thumping theatre, and squash you into second-rate sausage meat."

The response to his speech was resounding. A clanging and booming, a shouting and whistling erupted from the arena, and we were hit by a hail of apples and nuts, rotten eggs and tomatoes. "Do it, do it, do it," grunted the apprentices.

Burbage was furious. He swung his sword from its

scabbard and started to scream: "You bird-brained bleth-erskates, you grog-fuddled grocers, you wouldn't know a play from a piddle pot if it was staring you in the face."

All hell broke loose then, and dontcha just know it, I was in the middle, as usual. Lucky I still had my everyday outfit underneath cos my gown was ripped off and I was shoved into Hamlet's doublet and hose. They were so big on my skinny body they darn near drowned me. At the same time Burbage was stripped and forced into the tat-ters of my dress. His sword stolen by a groundling, he was totally helpless, and was besides bursting out of my bodice like a great ape at a fancy dress ball. I could glimpse his hairy chest through the rips and slashes, could almost hear the tireman groaning that he'd done the best he could with what he 'ad, but just look at the tangle we'd made of our togs.

At least now the crowd was moving back into the pit, ready to watch the play, and, barring the occasional catcall, screech, or drum roll, we were allowed, mussed up and confused, to muddle through the rest of the program as well as we could. We had a hard instinct that if we fought back we'd be firewood, and so, no doubt, would the The-atre. Burbage, the hot-tempered brawler, was sum-totally powerless for once, and, if I spotted a tear trickling down his beautiful cheek, I was gracious enough to ignore it. Besides, I was crying, too.

32

"Boy! Here, boy, here, bungling bat-eyed boy," Shaks-pere shouted right after the performance. Thomas trotted over. He'd returned the horses to their rightful owners and clearly thought my master wanted him. And when you think of it, he did fit the boss's description to a T. "Get lost," said Shakspere. "It's Willow I'm wishing for."

"Are you sure, Master Shakspere?" queried the doubter. "I was almost certain you were calling me."

"Why would I call you, you blithering backwards bean-bonce? Out of my sight, sirrah. Sling your hook if you know what's good for you." Thomas didn't move. "Evil betide you, bone brain, if you linger." The kid rushed off then, glimmering like a ghost in the twilight. "Here, Willow. Here, wet-nosed, whingeing Willow. Wasting my time as usual."

"Why don't you just doggam whistle, master?" I was pushing a broom around the stage, exhausted and fed up. I took my time setting it aside and walked slowly towards Shakspere. I'd known he wanted me from the start.

"Watch your mouth, sirrah, when you're talking to me, or I'll wash it out with lye." He eyed me up and down, his nose wrinkled with disgust. "I need you to run an errand."

"But I'm still in costume," I whined. And I was, too. Burbage's. It would mean a hefty fine if I was caught out on the street in it.

"Never mind that. You can change afterwards. Come over here." As soon as we shifted out of sight, I realized that the geezer was back to his rotten tricks again. He always whispered when he wanted me to do something devious. "You're to zip up to Vere's within the half hour, sirrah."

He had to have a screw loose if he thought I was going to run up there again. Especially on such a dreadful night. It was like Halloween and a swarming rolled into one, the last chance for the citizens to do some mischief before Lent. The streets were teeming with drunks, rioters, and thieves. If I ventured out, I'd be taking my life in my hands. "Not in this lifetime, Master Shakspere," I muttered disobediently.

"If you don't amble out this instant, boy, you won't have much of a lifetime left. Get my meaning?"

I shivered but stood my ground. "You can't frighten me any longer with your threats and menaces, you can't bulldoze me into doing your bidding any more, you smurfy old suck. I've made a mountain of money now. I don't need you. I can beat the odds on my own."

"This money, kid?" Shakspere held high a brown leather pouch, jiggling its contents with nasty joy. Yeesh, he must've stolen it from its hiding place under the straw mattress back at our house. I'd toted it along each time we moved, and guarded its contents with my life. Modulated muckrakers, a whole winter's work in the food trade, all those pounds, shillings and pence that I'd worked so hard for, stashed in his grimy hand. There was no way I could get at them.

"No," I yelled, jumping for the pouch. "Give me back my purse this instant." Shakspere took about as much notice of me as if I were a troublesome fly.

"All I need, sirrah," he went on, waving away my arms, "is for you to go up and get the cash owing so we can set about making new props and costumes over Lent. Because the men are gone tomorrow morning, many of them, back to their homes. They won't be in London again till Easter. They need a bunch of money before they leave so they can get going in the interval."

I must have looked lost. "For the play, Willow. *A Midsummer Night's Dream*. To celebrate the wedding of de Vere's darling daughter Elizabeth. To the earl of Derby."

He was spelling the whole thing out for me like I was a complete moron. "And then I may exchange the fee de Vere hands over for your pouch, and you'll be rich again. But for the time being I mean to keep it. As a kind of collateral. Not too much for you to manage, is it?"

I hesitated. Not even wealth was worth such risks. And I'd already clued in that, fetch the money from Vere or no, I'd probably never see my cash again. But the suck wasn't letting up. Glancing around, he repeated in low tones, "Not too much for you to manage is it...mistress?"

What? Gobsmacked wasn't the word. My jaw must have dropped about five feet.

"Oh, yes, Willow, tit willow, tit willow, don't come the innocent with me. I've lived with you long enough to know the truth. You might fool Rich Burbage, you might fool that young whipper-snapper John Pyke, but you'll have to get up a lot earlier of a morning to fool me. And if you want me to hold my tongue, you'll do as you're thumping well told."

Ugh! The creepy old geezer had been spying on me. No wonder he gave me the willies. No wonder he made my flesh crawl. Now I really needed someone to rescue my fat from the fire. And on top of everything, with no say whatever in the matter, I had little choice but to do as I was ordered and make haste to Vere's, petrifying as the prospect was. Because if the company found out I was a girl, I'd be out on the street, or worse.

"And one thing more, Willow. If his earlship should happen to hand you a...parcel...of the usual dimensions, make sure and bring it back to me safe and secretly, if it wouldn't be too much of a burden." The bald-headed idiot grinned.

"OK." I knew when I was beaten, so I gritted my

teeth and got going. But as I made for the exit, that bloated little pest Doubting Thomas hastened from some horrible hiding hole and slid past me. He'd clearly heard the entire conversation. And he was scooting up the lane and round the corner before I'd even made it through the doggam door.

33

Through the shadowy streets I ran, past bonfires, fancy-dress dancers, and drunken revellers. Once I thought I glimpsed Mistress Lewes and took off after her, managing to snag a sleeve, but as the woman turned, I realized it was someone else. An unfamiliar face loomed out of the dark, startled and angry. "Sorry," I spat out before speeding on. Your late landlady is lost forever, I told myself. Time you faced the truth. With no e-mail or phone to fall back on, no Internet to do a search with, I clued in only too well I would probably never clap eyes on her again.

What a nasty, miserable night it was, frost painting the bushes with white rime. Soon I was frozen through flesh to my very bones, and I queased with cold as I ran on. I finally made it to Vere's, through roads and lane-ways, chilled fields and furrows. But guess what? After all my trouble in getting there, no one even answered my knock.

"Hello," I yelled. Nothing, naught, nil. I examined the house carefully. Not so much as a lantern lit the windows. Not so much as a cat's tail crinkled the curtains. Bankrupt bungalows, the household had either all fallen asleep or the building was deserted. Where had Vere gone? I needed him right now or I was in major jeopardy. I banged and hollered, rattled the knocker and darn near kicked in the door, but no one came. Either they'd all gone deaf or there was absolutely, indubitably, positively no one home at all.

The night drew in. The dark got, well, darker, the cold colder. I had nothing else to do but sit shivering on the step feeling severely sorry for myself, while the glad sounds of merrymaking reached me from the village nearby. Dudes round about obviously let down their hair before Lent, and it was a dangerous time for strangers. The notion of making my way back to the Theatre was truly spooky.

But after a while, I gathered my courage and began the long hike home. After all, there was no point squatting there freezing my buns off. But I was worried silly, nevertheless, trying at all costs to avoid the villagers, and dragging myself miserably along the path. Shakspere would probably dump me for coming back empty-handed. He might even be mad enough to throw me into the poorhouse, and there wasn't a darn thing I could do about it.

What a bummer. I'd been fished out of the future, I'd managed to forge a life in this God-forsaken world, and now the whole adventure was collapsing, tumbling down around my ears. And all this time I'd been fooling myself there was a reason for me being pitched into the backwaters of time, some kind of meaning to the madness. Well, there wasn't. It was one of those dreadful accidents signifying nothing. I realized it now.

"'Scuse me, sir."

I jumped. A little along the road a small boy with a streaming cold was sizing me up.

"'Scuse me, sir," he whimpered a second time, wiping his nose on his ragged sleeve, "but are you here to visit the earl of Oxford?"

"Yes, yes, yes, yes." The affirmatives lurched from my lips like air out of a burst balloon. I took a closer look at him. Even though it was really dark, I could see the kid's innocent eyes, his curly carrot top. He checked out harmless.

"I'm remorseful for your trouble, master, but he ordered me to tell anyone who trouped by that he's moved to King's Place in Hackney. Mile or so east along the road. Bigly house. Mansion really. You can'st not miss it if you're mindful."

"Sorry, sunshine, but someone has stolen my purse, and I'm fresh out of cash," I said graciously, "or I'd give you something for your trouble." The kid shrugged and shimmered back into the shadows. I was on my own again.

Hmm. King's Place, Hackney. Mile or so east along the road. Even in the dark it'd only take me an hour at the outside. I just had to keep to the pathway I'd wandered down the last time I came calling, the night I went the wrong way. With no fog to make things murky, I'd hopefully make it to Vere's without a hitch. And just as I was getting so gloomy I was thinking of giving up. Amazing.

I was running along the path in an instant, filled with new faith. Doggam it, I would wend my way to Vere's new dwelling. And there I would talk with the posh, the powerful, the severe and somewhat scary lord. There was something important I just had to tell him. Something that couldn't keep.

34

I found the place without much difficulty. Carrot Tops had been right. The grandest house in the district, it was impossible to miss. I spied his lordship through a window, working away into the night, his face more than a little sinister in the candlelight. But before I spoke to him, I had to get past Bridget, who now cornered me with a vengeance.

"Fair Willow, sweet Willow, young stripling Willow, you've come to see me at last. How lucky I am not at Grandpa Burleigh's where I spend the primary portion of my dismal days." In a meeny mo her arms were tied round my stomach like tentacles, and she started jumping up and down like a doggam gymnast. There seemed no polite way out.

"Go away. I haven't come to see you at all, but your father. Bother your body parts. Get them off me, girl."

"But Willow, I want you. And I have news to impart. I am to be engaged to the future earl of Pembroke, but I would give up all for your favours."

"Darn and blast it woman, I have no favours to give you. Marry where you will, but don't involve me in it. And if you really want to do me a favour, tell my best friend that you're betrothed, so he won't spend all his down time daydreaming about you." I elbowed her in the midsection, and worked free of her at last.

"Next time I see him I'll be sure to tell him," she said stonily.

"Terrific. Now be a good girl and fanfare me to your father." Bridget pushed off with a scowl. I was announced.

Vere was still writing, scribbling a line here, a word

there, mulling over a muchly marked book. Crimson velvet binding peeped out at the edges. The Bible, I decided, eyeing the open silver clasps. Nothing else could be that thick and ornate. Barely brushing his eyes over me as I walked in, he scarce listened to me listing Shakspere's demands. He threw down his pen at last, crabbing, as he limped over to a cupboard, that my master was always angling for more cash, and did he think Vere was made of money?

"And perchance, Willow, you'd be so kind as to dispense this to that bubble-brained bumbler, that shuffling apology for a cretin, your boss." Handing me a parcel in addition to the money, Vere eyed his offering with regret, like he was sorry to see it go. As usual, a small black E and V were twined together on the outer wrap.

"Sir," I began warily, wanting above all things to wax honest with him, but a tad terrified all the same, "I have to tell you...it's only fair...it's important you understand...that I've fathomed your secret."

"And I believe I've fathomed yours. Stalemate." Vere wheeled back to his work, scowling.

"P'raps one of them, sir." What did he mean? Did he know I'd dropped in from the twenty-first C., or had he weaselled out I was a wench? That must be it, cos no one in their right mind would believe the other stuff. Sheez! Now it seemed like anyone who was anyone knew I was female. I must have grown up and out somewhere along the line. "How did you know?" I breathed.

"I've always known. You walk like a woman, you lisp like a girl."

"Oh I do, do I?" I flared at him furiously. "So why haven't you spilled the beans before now?"

"You never questioned my somewhat...irregular dealings with your knock-kneed snivel of a master, so I found it unnecessary and impolite to broadcast your sex. Besides, you made a pleasing and comely Juliet. Much better than those squeaky boys."

I swallowed hard and chilled. No doubt about it, it was a pain the earl had figured out my disguise. But though a day ago his guesswork would have provoked profound panic, I'd already realized as I rushed along to Hackney that, cos Shakspere knew the truth, the whole darn world would probably hear of it within the next fortnight anyway. His tongue could be loose as a bell clapper, and besides, the geezer hated me. He'd shown numerous times that he wanted rid of me. He wasn't about to keep his mouth shut about my secret. So it was futile to be freaked. Much more important, if I was about to be thrown on the scrap heap, I had things to do and say that just had to be done and said. "I've fathomed your secret, sir," I repeated firmly, back on track, "and I believe you're making a major mistake."

"And you would know." Vere paused briefly. "I never tried to hide the truth from you, Willow. I understood from the outset you had wit enough to work out the whys and wherefores. My nickname, Shake-Speare, given me at court, was similar to your master's surname. He started to pinch the plaudits meant for me, and I was delighted, borrowed him for a front man in fact, paid him handsomely to quiet the Queen's ire. She doesn't like it known her courtiers scratch out their livings with the quill. Nothing remarkable about that."

"I still say you've made a major mistake, sir."

His features darkened, shadows hacking into the hollows of his cheeks. Suddenly, he looked horribly forbidding. "Listen to the kitten minding the cat how to lap milk," he hissed. Picking up his pen, he turned his attention back to his work.

"I'm sorry, sir, but you have to listen. There isn't much time."

"Why, are there soldiers at the door? Has the Queen sent to arrest me...again?"

"Again?"

This time, he didn't even bother to look up. "I've had my fingers tapped by her highness before. Oft-times for my conduct, sometimes for my scrawl. I've been detained inside the Tower, and I should not wish to repeat the experience."

"Oh! No, sir. The danger lies in the future, but I must tell it now." I was shuddering, but managed to keep going. "Just think of Y2K."

"What?"

"Skip it." I thought for a moment. How d'you explain the millennium to someone from the sixteenth C.? It was hopeless, but I had to try. "Suppose you were alive and walking around, say four hundred odd years from now. Suppose you realized that sot, that saddo, that shambling stooge Shakspere was the best-known, the most written-about playwright of all time, just because you'd made him a present of your plays. Suppose those same plays were performed at every festival in the world, Shakspere called the wittiest wordster in a thousand years, while the name de Vere was all but forgotten, save for a fleeting footnote or two. How would you feel then?"

He threw down his pen. "That's a mountain of supposition, but I am bound to say if there were such a scenario, and I was to know of it, I should be well satisfied."

"Satisfied?" I couldn't believe my ears.

"Yes, mistress. It is a lame excuse of a nobleman who pens performances for the common herd. Though I cannot help but write them, I certainly should not wish to be remembered in that regard."

"What?"

"Edward de Vere, seventeenth earl of Oxford, has his reputation to consider. He is not about to be pilloried for a play."

"Why, you silly stuck-up sad sack of a snob! You think you're the be all and the end all, don't you? "The words spurted out of my mouth before I could grab them back.

"I am that I am." His eyes were blazing as he got up for a second time and limped to the library door, lungeing it open. "Now get out. I have nothing further to impart to you. And make absolutely sure that both my new work, *Cardenio*, and the payment for the players make their way to your master. It seems to me I shall need to find some other method of communicating with him in the future."

"You clued-out pen pusher! You mused-out mule! I came to ask you to claim your own fame. Why should shamble-butt Shakspere corner all the praise for work that you've done? But now I don't give a good doggam." That was a lie. I did care, very, very much, I just couldn't help myself. "You'll be stunningly sorry," I said stupidly, "after you're dead."

The door slammed. My words echoed eerily along the entranceway. I'd burnt all my bridges. Not a single one still stood. Riddling rotator cuffs, I'd dealt the cards too casually. Now I was out of favour, and I'd bet a pound to a pykester there'd never be a second chance to try to persuade Vere to come clean and reveal his true ID.

35

I hid the money in my double-size doublet, but there was nowhere to conceal the play. Meddling microcosms, I now had in my possession a parcel that was majorly meaningful to man (and woman) kind. At least one guy, the devilish Gabe, would give his eye teeth and probably his right hand for it, and there it was hanging out in the open air for anyone to see.

Cardenio. I'd never heard of it. Sounded like some sort of scent, some kind of paltry perfume. Question was, what should I do with it? Take it to Shakspere as I'd promised? or do the dangerous thing, pocket, in a manner of speaking, both play and purse, then try to get by in the city as well as I could alone? Unable to work out the best course of action, I decided to head for home, trying to winkle out a solution at the same time.

Dark and light. Black sky and bonfires. "Whither go you, wayfarer?" called out a peasant.

"Do not worry yourself on my account, sir. I wend my way toward London." I slid away silently, passing in and out of the shadows, crossing from one pool of night to another. Soon the Shrovetide revels would give way to Lenten woe, and the commoners would rise and go to church, every one of them repentant, all bells, books, and candles. If only I lived that long. Scared I'd. be sucked into a swarming like a tree into a tornado, I flitted along beside walls and fences, avoiding the riffraff as much as possible.

What was that? As I rounded onto Shoreditch, something familiar caught my eye. My leggings, my shirt, my twenty-first C. vest, all dressing up a big spotty boy about to burst out of them. "Hey there, ho there, kind sir," I nattered gallantly, galloping out of the gloom, "Good Shrovetide to you. Pray tell me where you got those togs."

"My ma got them down the market. Great, ain't they?"

"Entirely ravishing. But a bit on the small side, wouldn't you say?"

"Yup. I'm a gigantic goose egg of a guy, Ma tells me." Twisting his collar in his plump paw, he gave a mighty chuckle. I couldn't help but notice the pimples on his chin, the blisters down his neck, disappearing under his...my... shirt. Yuck.

"Well, see here, sir, a stroke of luck has come your way. Your clothes are too little, mine too large, so I'll do you a swap. Fair exchange is no robbery, as they say, and my attire is fit for a king." Yeesh, the tireman would skin me if he ever got hold of me. Stage costumes were like gold dust. I didn't want to think about it any more than I had to.

"But your doublet's devilled with eggs and other sloppy stuff. What's in it for me?"

"See here, groundling..." I replied, ready to punch him. But as he sniffed nastily, offended by my words, I minded he was a mile and a half taller than I'd ever be. So I chilled. "Excuse me, sir," I went on, "but the doublet will come clean with a damp cloth, and I will slip you, entirely over the top and with absolutely no strings attached, a shiny bright shilling for your trouble." Without hesitating for a second, I pulled the payment out of Vere's pouch. In for a penny, in for a pound...or at least a twelve pence, the Pykester always said, and anyway, it seemed to me I couldn't get into any worse trouble than I was in already.

But Sheez, now I'd thought of him, how I wanted to see John Pyke's lovable face. I was wasting away without

117

him. He could help me. He could get me out of a mess that was growing more complicated by the minute. If he wanted to, that is. I was missing him big time, and to think I hadn't even realized it till this minute.

"All right," mumbled Mother's Boy. "Turn your back so you can't see me change." That suited me fine. In a second or three we'd stripped off and were dressed in each other's togs. His hand-me-downs reeked. He couldn't have washed in a week of Wednesdays. Still, I was thrilled to have my own clothes back, no matter how bad they smelled, no matter where they'd been.

"Just one more thing, mate," growled Grim Weed. "Pass over your purse or I'll slice your ruddy belly open." Dwindling dingbats, would you credit it? Give a guy a hand and he'll take a doggam arm, or in this case, a stomach. And up to the moment he'd flung round and flashed his dagger, I'd thought he was the loser.

"Show me the money," he yelled, mad as a hornet. So what could I do? Not about to have the moron mash my midsection, I handed over the loot. He didn't wait around for an encore but made off with it in a moment.

Without Vere's payment, I knew I was doomed, demolished, done for. Shakspere would be sure to throttle me. If he ever found me, that is. I picked up the play and darted into a doorway to sit and shiver out the evening, trying not to faint at the awful aroma coming from my clothes, and wondering what the heck to do next. Cos there was no way I wanted to (1) end up missing like Mistress Lewes, or (2) stumble round the sixteenth C. till I was hauled off to the poorhouse or hanged as a bum.

What about telling the whole story to Burbage? Could I trust him? He was friendly and huggable, but too hotheaded. Will Kemp? Woe! No! The wriggler was out. Another notion...now I had my own clothes back, couldn't I try bombing over London Bridge to see if some walloping great wind or another dose of millennium magic would tumble me back to my own time? But what if it didn't, and I was stuck on the other side of the river when Beavis and Butthead sauntered by? They lived and worked there, and they'd defend their territory to the death. Even worse, suppose Gabe Spencer happened along? I knew he was more than ready to fry my bacon, and didn't want to give him the opportunity. No, I needed to shore up my strength before attempting anything half as hazardous. So what was left? Holy canolli! The Pykester! If I limped along to his home and blurted out my terrible tale, perchance he'd take pity. And if he didn't? I wasn't about to dwell on that.

This had to be the worst, the longest doggam night of my whole life. Cos just as I made up my mind and set off for St. Mary Aldermanbury, who should I bump into but that snivelling little snipe Thomas, speeding round the laneway and practically barrelling into me? "Well, if it isn't Weeping Willow," chirruped the kid. "Cheer up, sirrah. There's someone around who is just dying to see you, ready to even your score." Before I could escape, before I could even blink, the kid stuck his fingers in his mouth and whistled long and low, like a freight train going through a tunnel. In an instant grisly Gabe Spencer was standing in front of me, making like he was going to give Thomas a medal for the wonderful work he'd been doing.

So the little creep had been on the snoop from day one. No wonder the rival gig always knew where to find me. No wonder Gabe could always ferret me out. No wonder he was always on my case. Though there was still the same nagging question: What did he want with the parcels?

119

Right about then, everything happened so fast that I didn't have time to spit. Though I did twig I was well and truly trapped. Not a corner to creep to, not a hole to hide in. It was too darn late. I backed up, aghast.

"Give me the play, Toe Jam," growled Gabe. "Pay back time."

"No, no, no," I yelled, shoving up my hand to protect myself, and hoping against hope that a goodly citizen would hear me and come running. No one heard, no one came. "Leave me alone," I hollered hoarsely.

Gabe laughed. Metal glinted in his hand; his eggy eyes glittered with hatred. Arm hoisted on high, he screamed out in triumph. With a twist of the wrist he slashed slickly and smartly across my body, and I crumpled like a piece of paper. I felt a hot wetness in my breast, as if he'd spilled coffee on my shirt. Doggam it, doggam it to hell, the villain had skewered me. A dark stain was spreading in a satiny circle over my vest, the edges fanning further and further afield with every heartbeat. My parcel was peeled from me like a Band-Aid, and I fell to the ground.

"Why don't you write your own stupid plays instead of stealing Vere's?" I gasped, realizing at last what his game was. But Spencer had quit the scene, dashing round the corner like the devil, and that scurvy sneak Thomas ran away too, after gaping at my wound with disgust.

"Dontcha think you should finish him off?" he queried as he and Gabe shot off into the shadows.

"No time." The reply came hush-hushly. "But never you fret, the dummy's done for." Charming! Meanwhile the gathering crowd was staring at me like I was some kind of street entertainment. Yeesh! Now the Pykester really had to feel sorry for me. Mayhap I honestly was on my last legs. Perchance I was dying. I almost fainted at the thought. My enemies, Shakspere, Vere, Spencer, were stacked against me mountain-wise, and I was withering under their weight. Slowly and muchly, muchly sorely, I pulled myself upright. Avoiding the crowd, who had no intention of helping me anyway, I faced west, and grabbing hold of a wall, began the long limp towards John Pyke's lodgings.

36

"Hell's bells, what hit you?" muttered my ex-pal, as Blossom licked my face. As soon as he'd seen what had happened, as soon as he'd spotted the spreading scarlet stain, now ringed with ice from the wretched weather, the Pykester had relented, dragging me up the stairs and onto his cot. He flared a candle in his little breadbox of a bedchamber, the flame lighting his lovely face. The rest of his household, the Heminges family, were in bed, either counting sheep or sound asleep.

"A doggam Mack truck. No, forget it," I whispered, gazing into his gorgeous baby blues, which for the nonce were full of sympathy and upset. "I was caught in a squabble or three, and only won two of them."

"I'll stir Mistress Heminges. She'll know what to do."

"Wait, Pykester. Lend me your ears. There's something of much import, a vital secret I just have to tell you...right away. You know I keep running off to Vere's? And you know the plays, Shakspere's showpieces?" I could barely speak. An overwhelming weakness kept messing up my words. And the straw under John Pyke's sheet was sharp as needles in my back. This must be how the princess felt when they shoved a pea under her mattress.

"Can't we delay this discussion?" The Pykester was fussing round me like a mother hen while brooding over the bloody spot. It was waxing wide as the Red Sea.

"No...can't...please listen." Painfully, I moved closer to him. The room was shimmering, switching on and off like Christmas tree lights. Now I could see his discarded jerkin, the little bureau in the corner, the wobbly three-legged stool. Now I couldn't. Now his fair hair was coming and going in a whir of angel's wings. His voice swelled and dipped. Feeling desperately seasick, I grabbed his arm. I tried to speak, but he stopped me.

"If you're going to tell me the earl of Oxford wrote the plays and Master Shakspere's his henchman, I already know that, so you'd be wasting the little breath you've got left. Now let me rouse my landlady before you faint on me."

"You know?"

"Willow, the secret of de Vere's writing is like a little locked box to which everyone has a key. We've all known forever. I know, Burbage knows, Kemp knows, Heminges knows. Judging by the way you were, well, waylaid before Christmas, the rival gig knows as well. It's a great gossipy game. But we're really careful as far as Wannabe Will is concerned, for he'd have a horrible hissy fit if he knew we knew, if you catch my drift."

The final piece of the puzzle! And what a whammy! Now, once and for all, I understood how Gabe Spencer knew I was carrying something, why he was always on the grab. To think I'd been running up to Vere's and back again, risking my health, heck, risking my life to keep the secrets of that rat-tailed imbecile of a Shakspere, when all the time it was a complete waste of time and energy. Everybody knew.

"Why didn't you tell me?"

"I probably would have gotten around to it if I hadn't thought you were making nice with Bridget."

"What about Vere?" I whispered. A reddish smear stole slowly across the sheet. Maybe I really was about to die. The whole sordid scenario was scaring me silly.

"What about him?"

"Has he figured out you all know?"

"I think so. But he doesn't greatly care. As long as his name doesn't appear on the plays, as long as the Queen's content, he's seemingly sparked. Though he does pretend to keep the whole affair secret, and he can act semi-scary if someone ruffles his feathers. Which Master Shakspere always does. He's forever putting the squeeze on de Vere, demanding more cash and plays. I'm sure some days the earl wishes he never got mixed up with him in the first place." Pykester paused and looked at me. My face must have been as white, or mayhap grey, as the sheet I was lying on. "Listen, I'm out of here. Going to fetch help before you seriously succumb."

"One more moment...just one, Pykester." I held on to him tightly. The whole doggam house began to tip. "This is so important." I was kind of panting now, the air coming out of me in little raspy gasps. "You have to do me this one favour, the biggest boon in the entire world, and then you can go fetch whoever the heck you want to. Mistress Heminges, the apothecary, the priest, the doggam under-taker, anyone."

"Well, spit it out, then." John Pyke was jumping around in a sweat of panic.

"You've got to pledge to me, Pykester, you've got to swear. You have to promise, have to avow that if something horrific happens to me you're going to make sure Vere's name is written in big letters on the cover of his plays."

"Sheez, Willow, the dude would kill me for less."

"No, Pykester, you're going to pledge. It's crucial. Wait around till he dies if you have to, delay until after his funeral, but would you please see it's done? He'll bless you...in heaven, I just know it...and so will I. That's the reason I was beamed back here, into this blathering backwoods of a world. I know now."

"OK OK," agreed John, distracted. I wasn't even sure he knew what he was swearing to. He just wanted to get out of that bedchamber in a hurry and find someone to stop the bleeding. When we'd done talking he was out of the room so fast I could feel the cold breeze billowing back on my head.

"Thanks, Pykester," I whispered weakly, "I owe you one." Blossom still hung over my pillow, her little red lollipop of a tongue licking my cheek. I patted her on the paw. "Sorry I kicked you that time, pooch," I whispered, just before everything went black.

John Pyke

Lent, 1596. At my door in the darkest of the night, Willow, his doublet black with blood. Removing him to my chamber, I wish to go and wake Mistress Heminges immediately, but the little one is full of idle chatter, will not release me till he says his piece.

His countenance pale as the snow without the house. Him weak as a kitten, frighted as I've ever seen. Moving to brush away the blood, I realize once and for all, from the cut and crease of his shirt, that Willow, mercy on us, has ever been a clever counterfeiter of manhood, a true and comely wench.

Now, distracted, I hear nothing she says, cannot stay, afeard by the deadly danger to her very survival. Running to rouse my landlady, I return to find the girl gone. Not a wrinkle, not a trace of carmine on the bed to attest to her former presence. "A nightmare," murmurs Mistress Heminges, "brought on by all the rich delicacies and a skinful of shoddy ale." But how is it possible? I have seen the young one with my own eyes, touched her fevered brow, my arm held hardy in her lily hand.

Now all is turned on its head. Willow returns not. Thomas tries out for Titania. A play is lost. Shakspere is badly out of his humour. It has been bruited also that the earl of Oxford has become reclusive, keeps only to his house, vicious-mouthed and foul-tempered, penning verse to a dark lady.

Methinks Willow assigned some sacred duty to me before leaving, made me pledge a promise I soon forgot in the heat of the horrid moment. I rack my brains, yet cannot recollect. But of what possible import can it be now? She is gone, merciless heavens, she is gone. Too late I understand her fondness for me, recognise she is worth a dozen dozen ladies of the court. I live my life remembering. Amen.

38

I opened my eyes. Doggam it, where was I? Lying on the sidewalk by the Thames, I realized. Mel and Sam were hanging over me, their purple and orange mouths flapping like they were a couple of fish out of water. They were yelling at me, I guess, but I couldn't hear them, could just see their lips waving while I lay in a daze. Smithson was there too, and seemed intent on bashing me into more of a stupor. No, I tell a lie. She was practising some kind of torture meant to bring me round. "Hey, stop it," I cried, cos whatever the manoeuvre was, kiss of life or artificial respiration or whatever, it hurt like you wouldn't believe.

The sky was grey as graphite, the river silvery. Pedestrians were making their way along the footpath like it was just a normal day. A crowd gathered round me, my class and some of the homeless kids from under the bridge. Gradually I realized that I'd been pushed forward to the twenty-first C. It was like turning the TV back on after a blackout. In some way I couldn't fathom, I'd winged it across four hundred years, besides travelling over to London Bridge from the Pykester's house in St. Mary Aldermanbury.

"Perin, what the hell happened to you? We've been searching all over," said Sam. Perin? Right, that was me. It was so long since I'd answered to that name I barely recognized it.

"You must've fainted," she went on.

"And you stink like you tumbled into the Thames. Pooh," grumbled her friend. Sheez, they really were like two of Macbeth's witches. All they needed was a broomstick or three, and two of those high black hats. But I have to admit that though I felt truly sorry to lose John Pyke, couldn't imagine going on without him, I was really happy to see the two of them. Because they meant I'd found my way through the wormhole. I'd made it back to my own time.

I glanced down at my clothes. They did reek, perhaps from sweat, or from fear. And they looked like they'd been churned through a dirt-and-dust cycle in the washing machine. Not a bubble of blood, though, not a hint of a slash where Gabe's dagger dove in. And when I sneakily peeked underneath, there wasn't a trace of my sixteenth C. workaday togs. So the past couldn't have happened after all. Sheez, Sam was right. I must have passed out on my way to the New Globe, and dreamed, or rather nightmared, the entire episode. Hard to believe, but my film-starry John Pyke existed only in Nowheresville, a figment of my colourful imagination.

"Bye-bye, Pykester," I whispered, my lips as dry as Arizona. I dragged myself to my feet, wondering how I could have made up someone half so adorable.

"Better get you back to school," said Smithson sharply, as she grabbed my arm. I felt like I was under arrest. "A hot bath, a meal and a sleep, and you'll be good as new in the morning." A sleep? What the heck else had I been doing? But I was tired out, it was true, and only too glad to hop into my little dorm bunk and lose consciousness.

And next day, I have to admit, things did look a whole lot healthier. Wow! A shower! A toilet that flushed! Optimal! But I wasn't sure I was ready for a day in the classroom, where nothing, sad to say, had changed. The sun was still struggling to shine through the filthy windows, Mel and Sam were still griping about the course, and Pete

Cross was still earnest as a preacher at Easter. But pounding the bard into our heads had become a horrible habit for Smithson, and she wasn't about to change. "Turn to page 145 of your *Macbeth*s, people."

I picked up the book and was about to flick through it when something on the cover stopped me cold. I couldn't believe my doggam eyes. Under the title, clearly printed in gold and green, was the name Edward de Vere, seventeenth earl of Oxford. His name didn't rock or roll, squiggle or jiggle, though both my stomach and the room did. Edward de Vere. Vere. My former friend and foe. Rightfully recognized. As the writer of this play at least, and probably all the others.

"We'll take up where we left off last day. If you're feeling all right, Perin, perhaps you would read Lady Macbeth's speech, top of the page."

"Out, doggam spot," I read. Doggam spot? Didn't that used to be damned spot? Where else would Vere have got that newfangled curse from but yours truly, or from the Pykester, who'd picked up my word-quirks like a disease? I was struck speechless. Couldn't continue. Held onto my desk like I was about to be hurled into the heavens. Or maybe back into the bygone.

"Get on with it for heck's sake, Perin. We don't want to wait the whole day for you to dawdle through de Vere. We have things to do." Mel whipped out a mirror and began to heap on the makeup. "I never feel right till I've done my eyes," she confided, piling on eyeshadow while the room spun round like a, well, roundabout.

"Feeling a bit sick, Perin? Take a peck at my pykester. I always carry one in my backpack for emergencies," hissed Sam.

I was ready to barf when Pete Cross jumped up and

began yapping in that stuffy way of his. "But Miss Smithson, I heard de Vere didn't write the plays. *The Tempest* couldn't have been written much before sixteen ten, and the earl was long dead by then."

Yeah, right. Someone had got his dates wrong. I didn't get the chance to argue with Pete, though, cos Smithson chimed in, as soon as he'd finished speaking, "Edward de Vere is the greatest writer in history, and you'd do well to remember that, Peter. All these stupid conspiracy theories are just that—stupid."

"Why don't you just can it, Cross-Eyes?" Mel was now loading on lip-gloss and painting her lashes purple. They spiked out from her lids like the greasy spokes of a bicycle wheel.

"I know that someone was the greatest writer in history, but I'm not sure at all that it was Edward," Pete persevered, ignoring her completely. "In fact there was a little-known player in London at that time...Will Shakspere..." On and on and on. He didn't let up for a second. It was all so familiar, except the names had changed places. Weird!

"Now class, we'll study till eleven thirty, then you can take a break before we take the underground to Westminster Abbey to visit the tomb of Edward de Vere, the most phenomenal playwright ever." Thanks be to Smithson. Everyone groaned but puddled down to work, with the possible exception of the terrible twins, and I had a second or three to mull things over.

Everything must have taken place just as I remembered. Not a dream. Not virtual reality. It had all actually occurred. I truly had been propelled into the past, and somehow I'd managed to get the train back on the rails, restore history to its rightful course, before whisking back forward, if you get my drift, through the time warp. Now everybody, even those two idiots Mel and Sam, knew the truth about Vere. It was breathtaking beyond belief. Astounded,. I gave myself a mental high five.

After lunch I begged off the trip. To tell the truth, I'd had enough of the earl alive to last me a lifetime. I certainly didn't need to see him dead, examine his epitaph, his earthly remains. When all was said and done he'd turned out a pretty miserable old moper, mean and creepy. It was far-out to think that even though he needed a personality transplant, he was the one who did such a great job on the plays. And it was wild to remember that at one point I'd actually craved his good opinion. Now his approval meant less than a finger snap to me. But I did badly want to know how everything turned out for the other guys I'd met on my travels.

Pleading sickness, I waited till the others had left, then scooted over to the library. And after a good deal of searching, burying my face in mouldy old books like a pig rooting for acorns, I did manage to uncover some information. Ben Jonson finally killed Gabe Spencer, the ghastly grumbler, in a duel, squabbling over a play. Jonson was never punished for it, which was quite fair, I guess, taking into account what an evil monster Gabe was. *Cardenio*, that Gabe had stolen from me that night, was lost forever. Sad-sack Shakspere trotted back to Stratford right after Vere died. I suppose the game was up by then, and he had no one to front for any longer. Bridget never actually married her earl. Well, served her right. She didn't love him anyway.

Of John Pyke, my beloved Pykester, I couldn't find anything rumoured or writ after he left the Admiral's Men, long before I ever collided with him. But I'm sure, I'm just about certain he had to be the one who did me a favour and broadcast the bard's true name to all the nobles and knaves in Christendom, after Vere succumbed to the plague. It wouldn't be Vere himself. He was too darn pig-headed. Too smug. Too stubborn to change his mind. Oftentimes, in fact, I can't figure out why I worked so doggam hard to get him the respect that in most ways he didn't deserve.

No, John Pyke had to be the hero. It was a no-brainer. With that winning grin and those cute baby blues, how could he be otherwise? I'd bet my life he made good on his promise. He put history back on track, and I'll always adore him for it. I'll majorly miss him, too.

I have to go now. We're acting out a scene from the Scottish Play. I'm to be Lady Macbeth. And, unlike before, I have all the moxie in the world. Cos when it comes right down to it, I've had a bellyful of practice. As an actor on a real Elizabethan stage. Doing de Vere. The rest is silence. Heigh ho.

Afterword

With the exception of Beavis, Butthead, and Doubting Thomas, all the named characters from the Elizabethan portion of this book genuinely existed. Even Robert Goffe, an apprentice with the Chamberlain's Men. Even Mistress Lewes, whose brother figured in court documents of the time. They actually breathed the London air of the 1590s and, one way or another, they passed their lives in the company of the greatest playwright ever known—whoever he was. That is not to say they were as they appear here. In *A Question of Will* we see them through Willow's eyes, and Willow has a funny way of looking at things. She tends to exaggerate everything and treats almost everyone, except her beloved John Pyke, with derision. People may be a little irked at the way she talks about Will Shakspere, but, when you come right down to it, she isn't any nastier about Will than she is about many of the other characters, such as Bridget de Vere and Gabriel Spencer. The way Willow mocks Shakspere may just worry people more because he's an icon.

Some readers may also be upset because I, as the author, and therefore the one ultimately responsible for the book, am tinkering with the characters of real people, but Shakespeare did it all the time. He made Macbeth, quite an innocuous chap really, into a traitorous murderer and did the same thing to Richard III to please Tudor royalty. He fashioned Sir John Oldcastle into such a buffoon that he was obliged by Lord Cobham, an Oldcastle descendant, to change the character's name to Falstaff.

A Question of Will is comedic, and thus is prone to poke fun at people in various ways. In addition, the novel is structured rather like a Shakespearean play, with girls dressing up as boys, and romantic trials and triangles. Elizabethan audiences found jokes about disguised gender very funny. They also thought bodily functions, such as urinating and passing wind, were wildly hilarious, so I made sure to keep to the spirit of the times and feature them, too.

The message of the novel, nevertheless, is deadly serious. I honestly do believe that Edward de Vere, seventeenth earl of Oxford, was the author of the plays and sonnets. In fact I'm 99.9 percent sure that he was. Why only 99.9 percent sure? Because I'm never 100 percent sure of anything. But I have to say that many facts, previously hidden or unknown, point unwaveringly towards him.

We know much about him from his voluminous letters and early poems, and from what critics of his era said about him, e.g., that he was "the best for comedy"—although, if he wasn't Shakespeare, there are no surviving plays by him. He was well educated, with both university degrees and legal training; he lived for a period in Italy, the setting for many of the plays; his life in many ways paralleled the life of Hamlet and more particularly the sonnets; the verses underlined in his Bible match many of the Biblical passages quoted in the plays; and his nickname was Shake-speare. There are several other reasons I and many others, who are much more learned than I, believe de Vere was the true William Shakespeare. For a fuller discussion you might like to visit the Shakespeare Oxford Fellowship home page on the web (*https://shakespeareoxfordfellowship.org/*), or read Joseph Sobran's book, *Alias Shakespeare*.

The question then begs to be asked: why *don't* I think

that Will Shakspere of Stratford wrote the plays? Well, for a start, we know very little about him, and what we've learned doesn't seem to mesh with the writing. We're not even sure that he could read. There was a school in Stratford, but we don't have any evidence he went there. Certainly he didn't go to university or have access to the broad knowledge of the court or legal profession that is so obvious in the plays. His father, his wife, and one of his daughters were all illiterate, which doesn't bode well for him. And though we have half a dozen signatures of his, they are ill assorted, some spelled differently from others, some seemingly in different hands, as though another might have signed for him. His will, too, is rather curious, as there are no books bequeathed in it. Books were very valuable at the time, and we would have expected the Bard, who used various source materials, to have had many and to have bestowed them on his friends or family.

Shakspere was an actor and part-sharer in a theatre company, the Chamberlain's Men, and that is often held up by those who believe he wrote the plays to show he was a famous, clever man. But the position of actor or even sharer was not looked kindly upon at the time, as actors were not esteemed or even adored as they are today. In fact, they were often considered the lowest of the low, just one step above beggars. In order not to be arrested, they needed the protection of a company and the patronage of a high-born man such as the first Lord Hunsdon, the Lord Chamberlain. Of course, actors' standing in society is in itself not proof of anything, but the small parts we think Shakspere played, which are so bare of lines a nonreader could have learned them, indicate he was not even an accomplished actor certainly not, like Burbage, one of the leading players of the troupe.

I've tried to be as precise as I can about the period. The sixteenth century was so disgusting by our standards we would probably be quite sick if we, like the unfortunate Willow, were thrown back there. Although there were laundries, people rarely bathed (it was considered unhealthy) and were filthy beyond imagining. Almost everybody was infested with head and body lice. Houses and streets were piled high with garbage, and the entire city of London was overrun with rats and fleas, which were, of course, the principal cause of the plague that killed de Vere and thousands of others.

Yes, in answer to the critics, there were beer bottles in Elizabethan times, even though they may seem to us a modern invention. And yes again, Queen Elizabeth did live in a succession of dirty palaces, usually staying at Greenwich or Whitehall at Christmas. Although in her youth she was reputed to be extremely attractive, with an easy grace and auburn flowing hair, by the mid 1590s, according to at least one report, she wore a wig and had a mouthful of rotting black teeth, mainly because of her addiction to sweets.

The place names are all real and the descriptions of religious days, such as Christmas, Candlemas, and Shrove Tuesday, are reasonably accurate within the context of the novel. Servants were indeed given presents or "boxes" on Boxing Day. That's where the name of the holiday originated. Many a bear saw its own shadow on February 2nd. And at least one theatre burned to the ground on Shrove Tuesday, the night before Lent.

I have, I admit, made some changes to suit the tone and plot of the story. The language is not meant to be Elizabethan, only to suggest Tudor talk in a jazzed-up, hopefully funny way (at the beginning of the novel at least—afterwards the characters all become infected, to one degree or another, by Willow's modern slang, just as she is influenced by their speech). The actors probably didn't stay at the Cross Keys Inn or the palace. They just performed there. And the plays the Chamberlain's Men put on for Elizabeth during the winter of 1595 were not necessarily the ones in my novel. I have just chosen some of the ones that are more popular today, while paying strict attention to when they might have been written. A note here for those who abide by conventional dating methods: according to Oxfordian scholars, *Hamlet* existed long before 1595, so I have felt free to include it in the story.

I do hope you enjoyed *A Question of Will*. And I especially hope you will do further reading on your own so that you can figure out for yourself the answer to one of the most perplexing riddles of all time: Who really wrote the plays and poetry of William Shakespeare?

L.K.

About the Author

Author Lynne Kositsky draws on her experience as a teacher of English and Drama in *A Question of Will*, creating a modern story in pseudo-Elizabethan English. An award-winning poet, she has been making her presence known in children's literature. Her second novel *Rebecca's Flame* has joined *Candles* as a CCBC *Our Choice selection.*

Who wrote Shakespeare's plays? Kositsky dramatizes her take on this experts-only controversy in her outrageous romp through Elizabethan London—told from the perspective of a lost-in-time teen. The result is an unorthodox but effective presentation of the debate in a story that is both highly entertaining and informative. And, above all, accessible to non-academics of all ages.

The author, born in Montreal, grew up in England. She returned to Canada in 1969 and now lives in Toronto with her husband and two recently acquired sheltie pups. The Kositskys also have three grown children.

Critical Acclaim for Lynne Kositsky

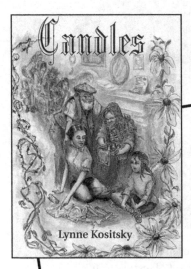

Candle One

I always hated being Jewish around Christmas. I couldn't help but notice that all my school friends were so-o-o hyped and into preparing for the holiday, and there was such a coming and going, a to-ing and fro-ing at their houses before Christmas Day. They seemed to have millions of presents to buy, cookies to bake, trees to decorate, and stockings to hang up. Meanwhile, I was bummed because all I had was Chanukah, which was a real bore when you compared its dim candles to my pals' brightly wrapped gifts and flittering lights. I liked their story better too—how can you compare oil burning eight days to a baby in a stable with kings,

Made in the USA
Middletown, DE
15 November 2019